SINS OF THE MOTHER

A Lexi Fagan Mystery

by Autumn Doerr

Books in the Lexi Fagan Mystery series

Baker's Dozen

Free For All

Sins of the Mother

Autumn Doerr made this story up. It is a work of fiction. The characters in this book are figments in air. Any resemblance to actual persons, living or dead, events and locations, is purely coincidental with one exception: the story of Lexi's friendship with Stella Brooks in the early 80s. Stella was a jazz singer in the 1940s during the Beat era in San Francisco. There is a digital recording of her singing available on Folkways.si.edu. It is worth a listen.

WGA Registration 2316833
© Copyright 2025, Autumn Doerr
All rights reserved.

ISBN: 978-0-9861209-5-4
Autumn Doerr, Pasadena, CA

Interior design by Pooja Mehra
Cover art by Joseph Stoddard
Author photograph by Gina Cholick
Autumn styled by Kim Apodaca
Location of photograph Found Coffee, Eagle Rock, CA

For the past, present, and future residents and visitors of Ketchikan, Alaska, my hometown. And for my Nucca Bill. We miss you.

*"You want to unknow, to erase, to start over.
Unsee the seen."*

- Lexi Fagan

TABLE OF CONTENTS

1

Ketchikan Ferry, June, 1987: Lexi returns home to attend her grandfather's funeral. As the ferry chugs along the Alaskan panhandle, she dreams about the defining moment of her life—the day her parents died. She was not even a year old.

It was not supposed to be like this. Her first trip back to Ketchikan after moving to San Francisco shouldn't be to attend her grandfather's funeral. On the deck of the ferry, Lexi was reading Sue Grafton's "A is for Alibi," picked up from the remainder bin at City Lights Books. Popular fiction wasn't for sale at the famous bookstore so someone must have dropped it into the bin. She smiled to herself as the salesperson peered over their reading glasses and rang it up anyway.

It was hard to concentrate. The last time Lexi was on a boat someone had tried to throw her overboard. And, returning to her hometown stirred a lot of emotions, sharpening the pain of her parents' absence and the decision to leave Ketchikan, to find a new path, a new kind of family.

The ferry entered the Tongass Narrows—the lane of ocean between the mainland and a string of islands that make up Southeastern Alaska. Lexi had missed a patch of Canada–the town of Prince Rupert–with her head in the book. It was cold and wet but she was determined to stay outside as long as she could before the rain started to pummel the deck. She finally gave up.

Now on a molded plastic bench cradling a cup of tea, she stared out the window. It was so wet with heavy mist that the world seemed to end at the railing as clouds enveloped the ferry. Lexi pulled her slicker close against the damp and tucked her curly hair under the hood. The engine's steady rumble drowned out all other noises like the rain obscuring the world outside.

The last time Lexi was on a ferry was two years ago. It was Halloween day and she was on her way to Sausalito to meet a man she had so wanted to be in love with. It was also the start of working with Detective Robert Reiger on police investigations who was now a friend and father figure. They shared a feeling of loss–Lexi having lost her parents when she was a baby and Detective Reiger's loss of his daughter to a hit-and-run accident when Jada was only 15. Their friendship as unlikely as Lexi's involvement in two of his cases–a disappearance and murder.

A lot had happened since she nearly became that killer's next victim. She picked up her book, pushing the memory away by burying herself in fiction.

Half an hour later, the mist, and her mind, had cleared. Walking out to the deck, she spotted an eagle weighing down a rain-soaked branch of a hemlock tree looking for prey. As its massive wings expanded and pumped the air, the mountain behind it came into view. Blanketed with pine and Sitka spruce like the hair of a sleeping giant, there was a bald spot, like a scar in the landscape, where the timber had been cut to make paper and cardboard. The mountains overpowered every surface of the waterway that linked the islands along the coast of Alaska. Trees lined the rocky strip of beaches that curved along the shoreline.

Lexi took a deep breath, catching traces of the mossy forest, the freshness of air after a rain with a hint of the rancid smell of the pulp mill at the edges.

Growing up, Lexi had not appreciated the majesty of her surroundings: 17 million acres of national forest, the largest in the country, had been her backyard. There were ancient glaciers, waters rich with fish and crab, timber as far as the eye could see, and vast oil reserves. The only resource now scarce was gold, long picked and sifted to dust.

It was a week ago that she got the call about her grandfather's death. Her grandparents, Doris and Brody, raised her after her parents died in a plane crash. Lexi called her grandmother "Gram" or "Doris," switching between the two depending on how exasperated or tender-hearted she was feeling toward her grandmother.

Doris was calm on the phone. "Brody didn't believe in banks, so I found money hidden all over the house." She paused. "Stubborn, foolish old man." Lexi could tell she was fighting back tears. "So, there's money for you to come up for the funeral and I expect you to be here."

"Of course, Gram."

"I'm going to rest my eyes," Gram sighed. Lexi knew it was shorthand for "this call is expensive so let's wrap it up."

A patch of sun seeped through the clouds, lighting up the deck. She had sat on one of the dry benches and closed her eyes. She must have drifted off because she woke up with a start, a dream of her parents coming into focus. A plane's wing dipped at a dangerous angle toward the ground. Lexi's father, Terry, looked at her mother in the pilot's seat. June was calmly checking her instruments, keeping the yoke in her tight grip.

Panic was rising in Terry's voice. "Did you check the gas tanks? Could there be a leak?" Trees and sky pinwheeled around them, the mountain dangerously close.

"I'm sorry," said Terry as June grabbed his hand, they closed their eyes as the plane collided with the mountain. Cold air rushed in as metal hit trees and rocks before the scene went blank and the radio went dead as their mechanic, Margaret, cried out standing in the hangar's office with static on the radio her only answer.

Flash to her parents floating in a watery grave.

Lexi gasped for air. She had had this dream before but never with such detail. She was a baby when her parents died and knew it was her imagination filling in her unanswered questions, but it never got easier or less terrifying.

Back to reality, something under the surface of the water caught her eye. Bubbles rose with murky movements from beneath. She shivered as a shift in the wind blew cold across her face. Looking at the dark clouds forming above, Lexi wondered, after all she had been through, if she had made a mistake coming home.

2

San Francisco Homicide Detective Robert Reiger is solving cases at a record rate, but his daughter's hit-and-run remains an open wound, unsolved and unhealed.

Sitting at his usual table at McCracken's Bakery, Detective Robert Reiger was taking stock of his life. He thought about his wife Jackie encouraging him to retire. He had 27 years with the San Francisco Police Department, had fought to become the first Black detective, and was tired of being the go-to example of Black excellence. But he was also damn good at his job.

He drank his strong tea and picked at his bear claw. It was hot for July. The old Mark Twain joke, "the coldest winter I ever spent was a summer in San Francisco" did not apply to 1987. A cold summer was one of the things Reiger liked about working in the city, but this year was a fluke, to the delight of the tourists.

He started coming to this bakery during a missing persons investigation. This is where he met Lexi Fagan. Once he trusted her, he realized she had similar qualities as his daughter Jada. An enthusiastic curiosity that easily turned into stubbornness and a strong will. This likeness resulted in a friendship that surprised them both. Even Jackie warmed to Lexi once the case was solved.

He drained his tea, left the bear claw half eaten, and walked to a table of acquaintances he met during the Jerry Stevens investigation. There was Stella Brooks, a tiny, old woman in jeans and a black turtleneck despite the heat. Henry, a retired PI, now in his late 80s who had fallen on hard times, and Tiny Timm, a little person with a sense of humor and a lust for life Reiger admired.

As usual, the subject turned to their mutual friend, Lexi.

"She's on her way to that town of hers in Alaska. It finally happened," said Timm. "Her grandfather shuffled off this mortal coil."

"Oh, Shakespeare is it?" Stella croaked.

"What was his name?" Henry asked not wanting to draw attention to his real question.

Detective Reiger answered, "Her grandfather's name was Brody."

Henry followed with a tentative. "How old was he?"

"Close to your age," Timm said casually until he saw the look on Henry's face and realized that Henry and Brody were the same age. "Just shy of 90." Timm knew that when someone dies at your current age, you do think of yourself. It was the same for Timm. When he read in the paper about a famous person with his condition dying, it made him shiver, even if, as often happened, they had died of old age.

They chatted about the weak coffee and how happy they were that Lexi had moved on from the bakery, despite the fact that the girl who replaced her was not what you would call friendly.

Detective Reiger glanced at the clock on the wall. 8:30 a.m. He said his goodbyes and left for work.

Though it was summer, the radiator in his office in the Howard Street police building was banging out heat. Reiger was sweating through his t-shirt to his dress shirt. He loosened his tie and unbuttoned the top button of his shirt. No air moved through the window, propped open with a stack of books. He wiped his brow with a hanky and dabbed his damp face.

Jackie thought he was overdue at the barbers, he had agreed that his afro and salt and pepper mustache and beard were longer than he liked, especially for the office where his co-workers felt entitled to comment on it.

His boss, Sergeant Stryker, wanted a report before noon on the latest arrest of a high-level cocaine dealer accused of murdering his girlfriend. He would much rather be in the cool morgue discussing the autopsy with Dr. Yu, but Reiger kept two-fingered typing on his Smith Corona. This was an open and shut case. The string of cases Reiger and his team had solved were starting to get media attention. The good news for the department also made Stryker look good with the Mayor's office, and meant that Reiger was left alone, at least for now.

Reiger wanted to finish the report quickly so he could follow up on a lead related to his daughter's hit-and-run. Jada was killed while riding her bike in their neighborhood.

Just thinking about the person responsible made his blood pressure soar. But he needed to think about something else. Something other than the image of his only child being driven away in an ambulance without its lights on or its siren blaring, her broken bicycle lying in the street.

He closed his eyes, focused his mind and saw Jada in their backyard laughing with joy as Jackie pushed her swing higher. He smiled as the old fan on his desk swung its way around, sending warm air into his face bringing his mind back.

The truth was, Reiger would not retire until he tracked down the driver who had killed his daughter. And do what, was a question Reiger did not have an answer to, but one he prayed on every day.

3

Lexi regains her land legs while conjuring up memories of her childhood climbing over logs, mucking around in creeks, packs of dogs trailing behind her and her friends as they race their bikes down empty streets in the rain.

The ferry slowed as it approached the dock of Alaska's "First City," the Southernmost port of Alaska. They passed downtown Ketchikan, a few blocks of bars and shops along the waterfront. An enormous cruise ship was parked at a deep-water berth off Front Street obscuring the "Welcome to Ketchikan" sign across Mission Street. This was high season and Ketchikan's deep harbor had four cruise ships docked right next to the town.

Houses dotted the bottom of Deer Mountain, scattered among the trees. Fishing boats docked at Bar Harbor unloading their morning catches. Tubs filled with king crab, decks overflowed with walleye, halibut, salmon, herring, and rockfish were stacked along the docks.

Front Street had bars to welcome a stranger and shops stuffed with trinkets for tourists. Outside the pharmacy, the white fur on the stuffed polar bear baring its teeth had turned a dull yellow, but still delighted newcomers.

Jutting up as if for attention were twin apartment buildings. The pink and green buildings housed the hundreds of workers pouring into town to work at the pulp mill.

Lexi's Ketchikan childhood was largely spent on a stool at the Frontier Bar drinking Shirley Temples with extra maraschino cherries as Doris and Brody ran tech rehearsals, Brody on lights and Doris on costumes, for "The Fish Pirate's Daughter," a melodrama put on for tourists every summer.

As a teenager, she had her first kiss while working her summer job at the Pioneer Home for the Aged. The staff were young and the residents showed more interest in engineering staff romances than pioneering.

There were good memories, but Ketchikan was the place her parents had died and the place she couldn't get away from fast enough.

As the ferry docked, Lexi felt dread over Brody's funeral. His death was one less thread to her parents, a connection that was already frayed. It did not help that she had a complicated relationship with her grandfather who was a "my way or the highway" kind of person.

It was not all bad. She was experiencing a whiplash of emotions. She was also excited to see her old friends. Colette, steady and clear minded, had a French mother and a famous totem pole carver father; kind and thoughtful Dot, also a native, was her best friend in elementary school; and Carl, the current Borough Major's son, was the only openly gay person she had ever met before moving to San Francisco.

Lexi, shuffled alongside other passengers down the ramp onto the old wooden dock. She spied a piece of what looked like fabric on the wet timber, a woven beaded bracelet. She picked it up and tied it around her wrist.

She felt like a San Francisco sophisticate wearing a raincoat instead of a slicker, Doc Martens in place of rubber boots. But as she took her hood off and let the rain run down her hair and into her face, she felt at once in her element and at home.

Doris sent Johnny, a family friend, to pick her up at the dock. Johnny did odd jobs and was married to her parents' best friend Margaret, the mechanic for the charter seaplane company they once owned. Especially since Brody died, Lexi often thought how odd it was that no one talked about her parents when she was growing up. Margaret and Johnny knew Lexi her whole life, but they never mentioned June or Terry. And, since no one brought them up, she had not asked. It was as if they had never existed.

After a quick hug and shy hello, Johnny loaded her luggage into the back of his car. He looked much older than she remembered, though his weathered face was still handsome. The rain beaded on his long black hair that he wore tied back in Haida tradition. It rained so often in Ketchikan that people rarely bothered with hats and would never bother with an umbrella.

After driving to the house in silence, Johnny unloaded her bags at the top of Edmond Street. She thanked him, handing him ten dollars, and stood on the street with her bags staring at the house. It looked the same. Painted wooden siding that had once been a vibrant blue long faded to gray. Empty flower boxes under the windows. A tiny window under the peak of the roof. The door, as usual, was not locked.

Lexi walked inside and slid off her boots. She could see Doris and her closest friend, Kak, sitting at the kitchen table in front of the picture window overlooking the Tongass Narrows. Kak was wearing her summer uniform, a colorful muumuu she picked up on one of her many trips to Hawaii. There was an island-to-island relationship many Alaskans had with Hawaii. Cold moist air exchanged for warm moist air, thought Lexi. Though she was sure it wasn't reciprocal. She could not remember seeing Hawaiians visiting Alaska.

Kak's long bottle-red hair was piled on her head, teased to within an inch of what physics could accommodate, bobby pins aided and abetted the look. They had opened the Dubonnet. "Hi," said Lexi, dropping her bags and joining them for a cup of coffee.

"How's my goddaughter!" Kak said, pointing to her cheek. "Kiss please."

Lexi kissed her. This was the kind of homecoming she had hoped for. As if she had come home from school and not been away for four years.

Kak, with a serious expression, looked at Lexi. "You look tired." Doris put down the paper she was reading to Kak and peered at her granddaughter.

Lexi, never knowing quite what to say to Kak's bluntness, responded, "Thank you?" This was pure Kak. She was a big woman who had panned for gold in her retirement wearing her signature Caftans. One of the few female lumberjacks. Kak had been close with June and was Lexi's godmother, but she and Doris agreed that Doris and Brody should raise Lexi since Kak was the kind of godmother who gave kindling for birthdays.

Kak was complaining about a neighbor who had suggested she put stickers on her window to stop birds from flying into it and injuring or killing themselves.

"Can you believe the gall?"

Doris leaned toward her granddaughter and whispered, "You know Mary Katherine. The only thing she nurtures is a grudge." Lexi smiled. Turning her attention to Kak, Doris said, "I have to tell you something." She often made announcements and Lexi tensed waiting for the shoe to drop.

"I had a donut this morning." Lexi's shoulders relaxed given that it was something trivial and not serious. "It's stuck right here." Doris pointed to her sternum.

"Doris!" Kak yelled. "Stop rattling on like an empty cart. Nobody cares where your donut has landed in your esophagus."

"Well you know it's going to give me gas." Doris protested.

Lexi and Kak said together, "Everything gives you gas."

It was good to know some things never changed.

4

*Detective Reiger makes a momentous
decision he can't share with his wife
Jackie.*

Detective Reiger was sitting in his car with the engine running and the A/C blaring. He thought that after all the years of wanting to know who had left his six-year old daughter for dead in the street, this moment would feel more satisfying and give him a sense of relief. But what he felt was dread. It had not occurred to him that he would be dredging everything up for his wife, Jackie. She had mostly been doing well except during the long hours of summer waiting for school to start.

Jackie taught 4th grade. It had taken her years to find the joy in teaching after Jada died. Did he have the right to shatter that? Besides, they always shared everything. Honesty was the rock in their marriage. Even looking for the driver without telling her was a kind of betrayal.

He imagined Jackie, her dimples creasing as she watched the kids in her class putting stars on their achievement board. Her hair pulled back, the hoop earrings he gave her gleaming. It was only three weeks until school started.

The conversation they had more often these days was about how overworked he was.

Jackie was sharp. "Bobby, you're getting buried by work, again." He started to protest but he knew she was right. Looking for the culprit, and keeping it a secret from the person he loved the most, had taken a toll on him.

"I'm not having you leave me, too, no matter how much work Stryker puts on you." She moved closer to him on the couch, putting her arms around him. "I fought the first time and I'll do it again."

He started to weep, wanting to tell her everything. That his buddy at the Oakland Police had a lead on a guy who had been joyriding in their neighborhood on that terrible morning. The news left Reiger feeling empty.

He and Jackie did not lie to each other and a lie of omission counted. He let Jackie comfort him before kissing her gently and leaving for work. For now, he would sit on the information.

5

Lexi reminisces about growing up with her grandparents. She discovers her mother's diary during a clean up following her grandfather's death.

Lexi was looking out of the picture window in the front room absently staring across the Narrows at Gravina Island. The scene was smudged with rain giving it the look of a watercolor. She could hear Doris and Kak talking in a back room.

It was warm for late June. The moisture and the heat created the perfect conditions for mosquitoes that swarmed once the rain ebbed. Lexi dreaded summer since she was a magnet for the blood suckers. It reminded her that there were so many things to love about San Francisco, including its lack of mosquitos.

Another thing she loved was that San Francisco was dense and energetic but was, and would always be, a finite 47 square miles. Where Alaska, vast and packed with nature, seemed endless. In the years since she left, Lexi lived in what felt like another country. She left as one person and returned as another. Now, she could more clearly see the history and the beauty as well as the stagnation of her Alaskan home.

Her mind drifted to the many cold damp mornings she stood in front of the warm oven getting ready for school. Doris attempting to tame her hair into Swedish braids weaved down her head and onto her back. By the time Lexi had tied her shoes, her curls had sprung out around their restraints. Her school uniform, a white blouse and pleated skirt, stayed mostly intact.

Lexi smiled remembering how the sameness of the uniforms was ruined by the chaos of her and her classmates' coats. The neat Khaki pants and starched white shirts for the boys and the girl's ironed stiff pleats covered by puffy purple jackets or long bright yellow slickers disrupted the conformity the church was trying to achieve.

Every school morning before she rushed out the door to catch the bus, Doris would crack an egg into the blender, add milk, vanilla, and a little sugar for an eggnog breakfast.

The smell of coffee brought Lexi back to present day. She breathed deeply, taking in lingering pipe smoke from Brody's evenings in the recliner and Kak's cigarettes mingling with cooking grease. Somehow it was all very comforting.

Looking around the living room, the sparse clean lines of Danish furniture were buried under stacks of books, old newspapers, discarded readers, pipe stands and handmade presents Lexi had given them when she was a kid.

Doris and Kak had moved to the kitchen and were hovering over the stove making Lexi a hot chocolate as if she were a little girl coming in from the cold after a day of horsing around outside. She half expected to see her grandfather lumber into the room and take a seat at the table. His absence hit her for the first time, but she would not let herself cry. Lexi did not want the ladies in the kitchen to fuss over her any more than they already were.

Kak brought empty cups and set them on the table; she was followed by Doris who poured the hot chocolate from a hot saucepan that spilled over and onto the spotted oilcloth, deepening the stain, a ritual that went back as far back as Lexi could remember.

Lexi felt a pang of guilt for having taken so long to come back. Expense was always the excuse but she could have found a way if she had really wanted to come home.

"The funeral will be short. No full mass." Doris said. "Brody hated church. We'll get everyone up to Kak's by half past eleven."

Brody had been just shy of his 89th birthday when his heart gave out, but her grandparents had always seemed old and were definitely ill-equipped to take care of a little girl. It was a group effort with Kak playing the role of Aunt and the editor of the local newspaper, Bob Kincaid, a friend of her parents, the occasional Uncle.

"I hate funerals." Lexi said, smiling to herself at the ridiculousness of the statement. "I suppose everyone does."

It started with the first she had ever been to at St. Paul's Church Cathedral in San Francisco's North Beach neighborhood, a full mass attended by the fire department in full regalia. It was impressive in a way but Lexi had been gutted to lose Jerry, and in such a horrible way. Soon after there were more funerals for her friends who had died from a deadly and fatal illness. It was little comfort that now it had a name, no longer the "gay cancer" but AIDS. Too many funerals with too much loss, she thought. At least Brody lived a long life.

They finished their hot chocolate in silence. Doris put the cups in the sink and motioned for the two to stand.

"It's time." They stood as she proceeded to hand out empty boxes so they could start to clear out Brody's things.

Lexi asked, "Isn't it too soon?"

"Nah." Doris said. She seemed chipper.

"You take the bathroom," Doris motioned to Lexi who headed down the hall, Doris on her heels.

In the bathroom, Lexi stared at the medicine cabinet—an ancient, rusted storage area for long-expired medications. The silver of the mirror had decayed leaving large dark spots so only part of her face was reflected. The way her grandparents had lived, their "if-it's-not-broken" attitude, had always amused her, but today she saw that it might actually have been more neglect and inertia than her bohemian childhood fantasy.

Lexi opened the cabinet door. Doris pulled out a bottle from a crowded shelf.

"What is the expiration date?" Lexi asked.

Doris put on her readers and peered at the bottle. "1962."

"Gram," Lexi lectured. "It's 1987. Throw that away."

"Not on your life!" Kak yelled as she came into the crowded bathroom and grabbed the bottle from Doris' hand. "Waste not want not." The bottle disappeared inside Kak's paisley caftan.

"I give up," protested Lexi. "I'm taking the attic." If she played her cards right, Lexi could avoid moving things from their house to Kak's. She decided, as long as she was looking, to try and find information about her parents. Perhaps there was a reason her grandparents never talked about them.

The attic was dank and smelled of rotting timber from the year-round dampness. It was getting dark and the rain came down in earnest making what sounded to Lexi like music as it hit the roof. Though she was technically home, a wave of homesickness washed over her, of what home, she was not clear.

She groped for the only light in the attic—a bulb hanging from a long cord attached to the peak of the roof. She pulled the chain and it blinked on, swinging back and forth casting shadows around the cramped room. Lexi had only been up here once before with Brody. He was looking for his purple heart for an Elks Club event honoring the volunteer fire department, which he had been a part of for 40 years before Lexi was even born.

She thought of her boyfriend Jerry, and how he loved being a fireman. She opened a large trunk, willing herself to set aside that tragedy to focus on another.

Old crocheted throws, threadbare sheets, a sleeping bag. She was shivering and pulled a stack of old Army blankets out of the trunk, putting one around her shoulders before sitting down and crossing her legs in front of the trunk. Underneath the linens, there were stacks of papers. An old playbill for "The Fish Pirate's Daughter," but no "letter to my daughter." Lexi realized it was foolish to think a letter like that existed, especially since her mother died so young and unexpectedly.

She pulled out handfuls of old clothes, handmade calico dresses, and a crushed wide-brimmed sun hat that appeared to be from when June was a teenager. She was surprised at how girly her mother had dressed. There was only one picture in the living room of her mother and father standing in front of the de Havilland Beaver bush plane, both wearing leather jackets and khaki pants.

When she reached the bottom of the trunk Lexi became overwhelmed, and wiped her eyes on her sleeve. What had she expected? With an arm full of clothes she rocked herself like a baby, the musty smell mingling with a flowery perfume scent. She wondered why her grandmother had saved them but knew if she asked, she would not get an answer.

"Lexi!" Doris yelled from the bottom of the steps. "We need you."

As she refolded the clothes and blankets, carefully returning them neatly to the trunk, a small book fell out of one of the blankets. Her hands shaking, Lexi turned it over. It was the diary. Holding it like a sacred text, she noticed a large locked clasp. This was no Holly Hobbie diary, but a thick leather bound book.

"Did you hear me?" Doris started to climb the stairs to the attic.

Lexi answered. "I'll be right down. Just tidying my mess." She heard Doris retreat and start talking to Kak about tackling the bedroom.

Lexi set the diary down and quickly stuffed more contents back into the trunk. Some papers and a small stack of manila envelopes slid onto the floor. Her heart beat fast as she opened the first envelope, quickly scanning the pages. They looked like official documents from Brody's military service. Discharge papers. Medical forms. Disappointed, she reached for the next envelope. Inside were yellowed newspaper articles. The headline on the top one read "June Fagan Becomes the First Lady Pilot in Southeastern Alaska."

The article was dated August 10, 1959. There was a photo of her mother standing on a dock smiling in front of a seaplane. The article covered Terry Fagan starting the charter service and flight school in 1955, Terry marrying June Barnes after teaching her how to fly and, subsequently, June joined the Fagan Charter Plane and Flight School. There was a brief mention of some kind of incident that occurred just after the charter business opened.

Lexi was jolted to attention when she heard a noise downstairs. It had gotten very dark, even the light from the bulb seemed to have dimmed.

"Lexi!" Doris yelled up to her.

"Coming!" Lexi closed the lid of the trunk, tucked the envelopes under her shirt and stuffed the diary into her waistband before descending the ladder. If Doris was not wearing her glasses, she would not notice the bulge under Lexi's clothes.

That night in her room, she set the diary aside. It had a serious looking lock so there might be a key. She opened the envelope and found a few yellowed articles, old scraps of paper, torn and missing most of the information.

She gleaned that a family had been on Admiralty Island and had scheduled a pick up with her father's charter company. A storm blew through the day the Sylvesters were to leave the island by floatplane. The second scrap of paper had information that Terry had tried to pick them up but the storm was too severe and he was forced to land and ride it out.

The byline on both articles was Bob Kincaid's. She quickly looked at the three remaining articles but they were puff pieces about her parents' growing business and the benefit to Ketchikan tourism. She read that her father had been an engineer before moving to Ketchikan. There was nothing about the accident that ended their lives, but she doubted her grandparents would have saved anything like that.

"Lexi!" Doris yelled from somewhere in the house. She had been home less than 24 hours and Doris seemed determined to root her out. She often snuck out to play with her friends when she was a kid. She thought, old habits die hard. There was no chance Doris would actually come looking for her so Lexi called back and returned to sifting through the articles.

These articles were a revelation. June and Terry were becoming more than ghosts. A young couple with desires, failures, successes. There was a diary. She wrapped it in a baby blanket she rescued from the trunk, imagining it had been hers, and slipped the article about the Sylvester family into her pocket. She had known Bob Kincaid her entire life and would ask him about it as soon as she could get away.

It was almost lunchtime when Lexi opened her bedroom door and heard Doris and Kak laughing.

"Brody was a pack rat!" Kak guffawed. "Look at these Playboys. And who needs 16 pipes!"

"Kak, clearly there are five." There was a pause and more laughter. "Wait, seven pipes."

Doris must have forgotten why she was looking for Lexi which made her feel very much at home.

They spent the rest of the day boxing up Brody's clothes, old books, pipe paraphernalia and most other evidence of his life, just like her parents. Once dinner was eaten and Kak had gone, Lexi asked Doris why she had never seen the articles about her parents. "Why didn't you talk about them?"

Doris sighed. "Oh you know. You were a baby and when you got older it seemed pointless to bring up the past. You didn't need to hear about how they died."

"I didn't want to know how they died, Gram. I wanted to know how they lived." Doris fidgeted with her cup.

Once the dishes had been cleaned and put into the drainer, Doris told Lexi to follow her. Inside her grandparents bedroom, Doris opened an old tackle box she kept her jewelry in, and dug around. She pulled out a necklace.

"This was your mothers." She motioned for Lexi to turn around and lift her hair. It was a delicate chain with a tiny ivory wolf charm. "Did she wear it a lot?" Lexi asked.

"Terry didn't like your mom to wear jewelry." Lexi wanted to find out more but saw how tired her grandmother looked.

"Thank you, Gram." Lexi felt the smooth ivory.

"Now skedaddle. I need to get to bed."

Lexi looked around her grandparents bedroom, now just her grandmother's. The bed was made. The bedspread smooth, the pillows in their place. Next to the bed was an old wooden nightstand. There were a few medicine bottles and an empty glass but no books.

"Where is your flashlight?" Lexi picked up the prescriptions and looked at the labels.

"It broke." Gram opened the top drawer and took out the old, heavy flashlight she used for reading.

"Are you sure it's not just the batteries?"

"It broke, honey. It got old like your grandpa and me."

Lexi felt ashamed that she had not kept up with her grandparents.

6

Needing a distraction, Lexi visits her old teacher, Sister Bernadette at Holy Name Elementary and runs into an old flame, Ross. Later, after dinner, Doris takes a hacksaw to a brick of frozen ice cream.

The next morning, Lexi was moping around the house unsure what to do with the information in her mother's diary and feeling gloomy about being home when Gram suggested she visit her third grade teacher.

"Go visit Sister Bernadette. Truly the ugliest woman I've ever seen. She's 100 if she's a day," she said. Doris had always been a bit jealous of Sister Bernadette. She and Lexi had been close all through primary school, and continued to see each other a couple times a year until Lexi left Alaska.

Lexi wanted to defend her against the "ugly" remark, but it was not far off the mark. Sister Bernadette had a fleshy face and watery eyes. But her compassion and kindness made her beautiful to Lexi. The sister had kept a protective eye on her. When sensing what she called "evil lurking," Sister Bernadette would blow her nose or rustle her habit to let the kids know she was watching, especially on the playground where older kids often teased Lexi.

Lexi took her grandmother's advice and caught the early bus to the school. Since it was summer, the halls were deserted. Red and blue construction paper with tiny handprints of turkeys and paper Christmas trees were still tacked to cork boards lining the walls, leftovers from the year before. The teachers would reset for the new year a week before school started in the fall. The cork board was always forgotten after Christmas.

The door to Sister Bernadette's small office was ajar. Lexi peered inside to see her resting her head on the desk, her arms folded in front of her. It was comforting to see a Kleenex tucked into the arm of her cardigan and a forgotten pencil behind her ear. It was as if nothing had changed.

The Sister was snoring softly, and Lexi did not want to disturb her nap. She sat in the chair opposite the desk. The noise must have roused the Sister since her head came off the desk and she looked at Lexi, her eyes focusing. She said, "I heard about Brody."

"I think everyone knows."

The Sister smiled. "It's not gossip I suppose, if it's a fact." She absently put on her reading glasses.

Lexi grinned at her. She must be pushing 90 and losing a step or two.

"Let me look at you." Sister Bernadette removed her reading glasses from her great nose and took Lexi's measure.

"You're quite fashionable."

Lexi always expected the unexpected from the Sister but even this surprised her.

"Classic 50s blazer. Tights. Doc Martens." She nodded approvingly. "And your hair. I like it back like that."

"Thank you!"

"So," Sister Bernadette leaned back in her chair. "This loss of Brody. It must be a blow, even though he was old, like me, and you expect us to drop off the twig."

They smiled at each other, unable to contain their glee at seeing each other after such a long time.

Lexi said, "I have a new kind of family in San Francisco, a family made up of friends."

"Like my church family." Sister Bernadette paused. "I get it. That's very good, but it doesn't mean losing a parental figure isn't difficult." Her face collapsed into a frown. Her large, moist eyes stared at Lexi. "Do you remember in third grade how you dug up baby trees at recess and brought them back to class. You had a little forest around the sink in the back of the classroom." She paused. "What do you think that was about?"

"I haven't thought of that in forever." She remembered the trees, the digging, the sink filling up with new baby trees. She laughed. "It seems weird now. I don't know what I was doing. Sister Judy finally put a stop to it and made me replant them in the forest."

"I think you do know what you were doing." Sister Bernadette took the Kleenex tucked into the sleeve of her sweater and dabbed her nose and wiped her eyes.

Lexi thought harder. The trees, small and growing. Baby trees. "I was saving the babies."

"Exactly. And the baby trees needed caring for."

Sister Bernadette stood up and gave Lexi a hard hug.

"Now off you go. You're lucky you found me here over the summer break." Lexi knew this was not true. Sister Bernadette could always be found at the school. Lexi blew her a kiss thinking this might be the last time she saw her.

As she walked the hall to the exit, she looked into the classrooms. Everything was so small: tiny desks in small rooms. Light filtered through the windows, the faint scent of chalk and the pungent lingering smell of children's sweat hung in the air. As she walked out of the school, she saw a handsome young man with a book sitting on a bench near the playground. As he looked up, a smile breaking across his face, she recognized him.

Lexi approached and asked, "What are you reading?" as if 13 years had not passed since they had graduated from elementary school. She gave him a proper look as they sat in the sun.

Lean, tall, and brown as bark, Ross's long black hair was loose around his shoulders.

He waved the book and said, "Bird Love" before folding the corner of the page and setting it down as she sat next to him. Though it was warm, he wore a heavy vest over a button-down shirt.

"I'm a teacher here," he explained. "This is the best time to prep for the fall," he said as he gestured toward the empty, quiet campus.

"I suppose you're here to see Sister Bernadette." It was more of a statement than a question.

Lexi nodded and said, "Remember when the nuns lost their habits?" She realized she was flirting and flushed.

"After Vatican II."

"Everyone took off the wimple except Sister Bernadette."

Ross pretended to strum a guitar. "Yet, none of them lost the habit of singing Kumbaya, my Lord, kumbaya." He sang the last bit, his voice like a clear bell.

Lexi grinned. "And Sister Roberta had a huge guitar. Almost bigger than she was."

"Sister Roberta is now married to Father Carlyle. Taking the habit off was just the start."

They sang in unison, "Kumbaya, my Lord, kumbaya." They were leaning on each other like they had done as kids. Lexi looked at Ross smiling and singing, his skin smooth, his dark shining eyes, and her heart broke open.

"I was sorry to hear about Brody. A long life well lived."

"How poetic. Thank you."

"You'll never guess." Ross said, excited. "I'm in the potlatch lodge ceremony."

"You're performing now?"

"I know." Ross leaned forward and looked back at Lexi. "I made fun of it when we were kids. You should come and see us."

The invitation made her smile even bigger.

For a time, they sat silently looking at the empty playground, shy, before Ross asked, "How is life in the lower 48? I hear San Francisco is beautiful."

"I love it. It is beautiful. I suppose I can't live anywhere that's not picturesque." She looked around at the trees and the mountains in the distance. "I don't like to talk about growing up here. Everyone thinks it's exotic. It's like I'm from another country. They ask what it's like and I talk about the totem parks and the potlatches and—"

Ross finished her sentence. "—And they are surprised we're still here. To most of the world, we're only ghosts."

"Out of sight out of mind. I didn't meet any Indians in San Francisco."

"We're not from India. We prefer being called 'natives' now," he said kindly. "We're hardly thriving, but that's changing. You should come to the potlatch. It's different seeing it as an adult." Ross shifted his weight and changed the subject. "Have you seen Dot yet?"

"Not yet."

"Collette?" Lexi shook her head.

"You were thick as thieves. Speaking of thieves, how's your life of crime coming along?"

Lexi looked perplexed.

"You. Dot. The Five and Dime."

"I can't believe you remember that. Our life of crime was short lived. We started with something small. I think I put a rubber ball in my pocket. Then when Mrs. Gregson didn't stop us, we started stuffing bags of marbles and candy everywhere."

Lexi realized she was staring at Ross. She felt like that kid in the store again. "Is the Ben Franklin still here?"

Ross responded with mock indignation. "Of course it is, city girl." He let his arm graze hers "You corrupted my cuz."

"That was the last time. It stopped the minute Mrs. Gregson told us to put it all back. I can't believe she didn't tell my grandparents."

Ross smiled. "She knew you'd be in more trouble than it was worth. You and Dot were all done stealing so what would be the point?"

"I wonder how she knew?"

"Speaking as a teacher, kids aren't sly. You weren't criminal masterminds." He chuckled.

"Is Mrs. Gregson still there?"

"No. Her husband retired a few years back. He was Coast Guard. They moved to Hawaii."

"From one rainy, wet island to another."

7

June's diary slash journal holds more secrets than Lexi can decipher. She visits the local newspaper and learns more about the plight of the Sylvesters and how her father fits into things. To her surprise, she reaches the daughter of the family that, according to the daughter, was left to die by Lexi's father.

Once home, Lexi went to her room to retrieve the articles she found in the trunk. She planned to visit Bob at the newspaper and ask him about them but Doris wanted her to go to the museum with her that afternoon.

It had not occurred to her that her 88-year old grandmother still volunteered at the museum and library. She made a mental note to call her more often once she got back to San Francisco, and smiled remembering how Doris would berate tourists with the history of the region and of the native population.

Still early in the day, Lexi disappeared to her room with a pair of pliers. She had not found a key in any of the envelopes she had taken from the attic so breaking the lock was her only option.

She mangled the lock until it eventually sprang open. Taking a deep breath, she opened the yellowed pages. Though she wanted to read every word, she skimmed her mother's childhood memories, which sounded very much like her own—endless summer nights playing with her friends in sunlight until all hours, choking on stolen cigarettes, riding bikes, and the rare sighting of the Northern lights. School crushes, her parents driving her crazy.

There were chunks of time June had not written anything, but there were also cryptic notes about meeting Terry, whom she referred to as "T." She wrote about how she pushed to learn to fly and get her license and his reluctance to teach her. Lexi was embarrassed at descriptions of their lovemaking that she skipped, trying to scrub them from her mind. The marriage seemed rushed, just after June became a pilot and joined Fagan

Charter. It occurred to her that her mother might have been pregnant with her when they married.

It was odd to think of her mother as a young woman still writing in a diary. She clearly had not trusted the lock because some passages were written in a code, which reminded her of her friend Carl, who always sent her notes in class that she was unable to decipher.

Looking at her watch, she realized that, if she didn't leave soon, she would sit on this spot and continue reading. Reluctantly, she closed the diary slash journal, as she thought of it, before hiding it under her bed in an old shoe box just as Doris called that lunch was ready.

Lexi checked that the article on Admiralty Island was in her pocket, wrapped her hair into a knot at the base of her neck, and walked downstairs to join Doris.

Grateful that her grandmother was reading during lunch, Lexi pondered what she had read. She now had a treasure trove of information, more than she had ever imagined. References to baby Alexandra filled several pages after months of no entries and an "R" popped up. There were a lot of meetings with "R" at bars. What on earth was her mother doing and who was "RO?" Another guy whose name starts with "R?"

Finishing her lunch, Lexi left. Her street, Edmond, had wooden sidewalks and her house was at the top of a long set of stairs that led into town. From up here, Lexi could see the two tallest buildings incongruously sticking out among the flat, low buildings of town. Two apartment buildings, the Pink and the Green, built in the 1950s to house workers from the pulp mill and their families. Lexi knew they had names, the Austin and the Wingren, but no one knew which was which.

The Pink building was where her friend Carl lived. There was that feeling of guilt, again. She had not called any of her friends since arriving, embarrassed that her correspondence had dried up over the years with the exception of a few postcards.

Lexi started walking down the stairs but stopped halfway at the Old Hospital where many of her native friends and their families still lived. It was a community within a community. The building was more dilapidated than she remembered. Paint was peeling from the window frames, there were clothes lines hanging mostly empty because it had rained overnight, the wooden walkway to the entrance was missing boards. It had never been officially turned into apartments and had a make-shift feel to it. There had always been discrimination against the native population over jobs and housing and her friends' families had little choice but to live where they could afford.

She continued down the stairs. On many occasions, she had tried to count them, but always lost focus after 100. At the bottom, she entered the newspaper's office, located in a square plain building. The editor, Bob Kincaid, was sitting behind a large desk covered in old issues, stacks of books, and photographs; large sheets of copy covered every surface.

Looking up, Bob said, "Alexandra!" He leapt from his chair in a feat of gymnastic wonder to give her a bear hug. He was still wiry and thin with just a little gray in his beard.

"I'm Lexi now." She says talking to his chest.

"Sure you are!" He roared letting her go and motioning to the chair in front of his desk he quickly cleared for her. "Sit. Sit." He sat down, grinning. "Tell me what you've been doing. How have things changed around here? What's San Francisco like?"

Lexi didn't want to be distracted from her mission. "I love San Francisco. Life's good," she paused. "But I want to ask you about my parents."

Bob beamed. "You are the spitting image of her you know? Except the hair. Those red curls are pure Terry."

"I need to know everything about them. What were they like?"

"Surely Doris and Brody told you everything?"

Lexi shook her head. Bob looked surprised. "Okay, I'll tell you." He cleared his throat then launched in. "June was courageous and smart. She was a quick study and was a better bush pilot than your dad. She was only 30 when she died." He paused to see how Lexi reacted. Her face remained passive so he continued. "Your dad was 10 years older than your mom. He started the business years before she came along, but she was the heart of the place once she got there." He stopped short. "I'm sorry. Should we not talk about their flying?"

"It's okay." Lexi gave him a reassuring nod.

Bob leaned back and sighed. "I thought the world of those two. I didn't grow up here, you know. Moved for the job as a cub reporter right out of college. Wanted to be the next Woodward and Bernstein but so did every other guy outta journalism school. So when a job came up in Alaska, I was all in. The 'Last Frontier.' Every man's fantasy. Didn't even occur to me that there's no news in a town without a stop light." He said with mock seriousness. "The crime blotter is lousy with 'drunk roused outside the Klondike Bar and driven home without incident.'"

Lexi waited.

"Your parents!" He said with a giggle. "We were young—this was before they had you—we all drank at the Sourdough Bar. Margaret, Johnny, me and Sally—this was pre-divorce mind you. We listened to music. We hung out with the actors at the old Frontier Bar after the play. Hell, we danced all night." Bob took a deep breath. "All that changed in 1965. The year," He paused. "You know."

Bob couldn't have been more than mid-50s if he and June were about the same age but she couldn't picture him, or her parents, hanging out with local actors, and especially not dancing. Bob was all arms and legs. His dark hair stuck up in want of a comb. Lexi thought he was handsome for an old guy.

"June worked for me part-time when things were slow at the charter business. She was an ace reporter."

Lexi's mouth dropped open, "What?"

Bob leaped out of his seat and headed for the door. "Come on," he said, grabbing his rain slicker and a Nikon camera hanging next to it. "Let's walk and talk. I need to get to the Coliseum." Lexi followed behind.

Outside, it had started to drizzle. Not wanting to miss anything Bob said, she left her hood down.

Slinging the camera over his shoulder he put the slicker on over it to protect it from the rain.

He continued, "Like I said, your mother was a smart cookie and had great reporter's instincts. And fearless! She uncovered the biggest scandal Ketchikan had ever seen."

Bob started walking with Lexi at his heels.

"June had been investigating the Mayor at the time, Richard Carter Shasta, who had a dirty secret. June had been tracking down information his secretary gave her."

"Just before the accident, June was chasing a story about Mayor Shasta. There had been rumors about him but nothing concrete." Bob repeated.

"Let's take the long way on Front. I want to check out the newspaper rack. Some bored teenagers have been stealing the papers." As they passed the Frontier Bar, Lexi saw the barkeep, Mary, sweeping the sawdust from the floor onto the sidewalk. She waved to Mary who gave Lexi an amused smile of recognition.

When she was a kid, Lexi and Carl, and many of the children in town, would sift through the old sawdust on the sidewalk and find coins and the occasional dollar bill. Everyone in town knew Mary.

When they reached the newspaper rack, it was half filled with papers. Bob gave Lexi a thumbs up and continued talking mid stride. They were walking fast and turned up Mission Street toward the movie theater. "I want to make sure this movie that's coming out gets to the Coliseum. Have you heard of it? It's called Dirty Dancing."

"No." Lexi stammered trying to keep up with what he was saying and with his pace.

They had reached the movie theater. Lexi had so many questions but before she could ask, Bob flung open the door. "Ralph will get the film for me." It was pitch black inside once the door closed. They stood in the foyer, the smell of stale popcorn and wet cigarettes the only sensation until their eyes adjusted.

Lexi said, "Can we get back to my mother and the mayor?"

"Sure. Sure." Bob said as he looked for Ralph. "June found compromising photos." Bob walked around the theater, opening doors as he yelled "Ralph!"

"We published the story before they even tracked down where Shasta was staying since his house was cinders. He was hiding in a shitty little cabin half way up Deer Mountain. The story was picked up all over the country. June Fagan had the byline." Bob didn't take a breath before yelling another "Ralph!"

Lexi said, "This happened just before the plane crash?"

"Yup."

A man walked through the doors to the theater and into the lobby. "What now?" He smiled when he saw Lexi. She put her hand out and introduced herself.

"Pleasure. Ralph Skaay" Turning to Bob he said. "What movie do you absolutely, immediately have to see?"

"Dirty Dancing."

"Do you think anyone's gonna want to see a coming of age movie that takes place in the Catskills of New York?" Ralph had shaggy hair and an untidy beard.

Bob looked hurt. "It's about dancing and freedom and l'amour. I'll write a great review."

"You haven't even seen it yet." Ralph shook his head, resigned. "Okay. But nobody, and I mean nobody, reads or bothers to follow your advice. Robocop puts butts in the seats."

"I'll write a review of that too." Bob snapped a photo of the Robocop poster, slapped Ralph on the back and grinned like he'd won the lottery.

Once outside, Lexi said, "Can I read those articles?"

"Of course." Bob said.

Lexi took the yellowed article from her pocket and unfolded it. "I found this in an old trunk at the house. It's about Admiralty Island."

Bob stopped in his tracks. He said softly, "Admiralty." He stared at the cruise ship docked at the harbor, his eyes losing focus.

He shook his head and looked at Lexi and smiled. "Like I said, you have a lot of your mother in you. I know a reporter at the Chronicle who told me about how you helped catch a killer." Lexi held her breath. She did not want Bob to go off topic again.

"You're a brave girl." He started walking back to the Daily News. "If you want to know more about what happened on Admiralty and that lake I can't remember the name of, there are follow up articles in the archives. It's all there. Mayor Shasta, Admiralty Island, the whole shebang. You could talk to Ruby Sylvester, the daughter. She's still in town but, be warned, she blames your dad for her father and brother's deaths. It wasn't his fault. There was a terrible storm." Bob waved at someone across the street. "What else did you find in the trunk?"

"Articles. A few pictures. My mother kept a journal." She was not sure why she referred to it as a journal but a diary sounded like something a child would write in.

Bob raised an eyebrow.

At the door to the office, he stopped. "I have a deadline but if you want to look through the archives, feel free. You can find Ruby in the phone book. Not sure she'll talk to you but you can get her side of the story." Lexi shook her head no. She did not feel brave enough to make that call.

He touched her shoulder gently. "Your friend Carl worked here for a summer after graduation so I know a little about what you've been through since you left."

"I was sorry to hear about–" Bob paused.

Lexi nodded, thanked him and headed to the archives in the back of the building. She started by looking for articles about Ruby Sylvester's accusations against her father. She found a mention of Ruby filing a wrongful death suit against Terry. The insurance company settled out of court. Lexi made copies of the article, and the photos of the Sylvester family and Ruby.

Lexi turned to her parents' accident. She saw the date, October 1965, written with a felt tip pen on a file drawer. Inside, she found the file for the 20th, the day after the crash, and pulled out the newspaper. Behind it was the Anchorage Times from the same date. It had been big news. She spread the paper across an old desk. It read:

"October 19, 1965. Tragedy strikes the city of Ketchikan when a de Havilland Beaver charter floatplane disappeared.

"The coast guard took off from Annette Island flying Sikorsky Seaguard helicopters and a Grumman Albatross to locate the impact area believed to be just off Point Baker.

The bodies of pilot Terry Fagan and his wife, co-pilot June Fagan, were recovered by the Coast Guard.

"The Fagans are survived by their daughter, Alexandra, as well as June's parents, Brody and Doris Barnes."

In Lexi's dreams, it was June who was flying the plane and Terry as the co-pilot.

There was another article from ten days later.

"According to Coast Guard Captain Paul Burwell, an FAA investigation has been opened. Captain Burwell stated, 'There were clear skies and no weather on the day the plane went down. At this time, there is no obvious cause of the accident. Unless evidence is found to the contrary, the incident will remain ruled as pilot error.'"

Lexi read the line again: "clear skies" and "pilot error." Her grandparents had lied to her. She knew her parents died in a plane crash but once she started asking questions at 10, 11 years old, their answers were vague and, now she realized, a way to discourage her from asking.

There were dates taped to some of the old drawers. Working back from when her parents died in 1965, she skimmed articles going back to '55 when her dad bought the seaplane and started the charter business but there was no mention of Jim's Lake. After at least an hour of slogging through folders she read about June being one of the first women to take flying lessons from Fagan Charter and Flight School, dated 1959, followed by June and Terry's marriage announcement.

She found the date and skimmed the papers looking for any mention of the Sylvester family being left on Admiralty Island. Bingo. August 7, 1961.

The headline read: "Family Stranded on Admiralty Island, The Search Continues for Survivors."

> "A family staying at a cabin near Jim's Lake on Admiralty Island, 195 miles north of Ketchikan, was stranded after the August 6th storm swept the region. Two of the three family members are still missing. Authorities rescued an 18-year-old girl, but have called off the search for the remaining two family members until after the hurricane-level winds subside.

> "Fagan Charter and Flight School, a local seaplane service, abandoned a scheduled pick up of the family when the proprietor, Terry Fagan, was forced to land and ride out the storm.

> "The names of the missing have been held by authorities until relatives have been notified."

There was a handwritten note paperclipped to the yellowed newspaper that read:

> "Follow Up: While Southeast Alaska is known for its precipitation, 1961 has been one of the wettest and stormiest years on record."

A second article gave more details. "Pilot Terry Fagan was forced to land on a lake miles from the island where the Sylvesters were. By the time a rescue helicopter arrived on Admiralty, the father and son, who were on a homemade raft on Jim's Lake, had died. The only survivor, Ruby Sylvester, was flown to Juneau, where the 18-year old is being treated for exposure at Bartlett Regional Hospital."

There was no mention of the mother.

The local story of the stranded family was below the fold. Above the fold Lexi read the blockbuster news from August 6, 1961, at the beginning of the space race.

"9:00 a.m. Moscow time: 26-year-old Soviet cosmonaut Gherman Titov was launched into space on Vostok II. Titov covered 17.5 orbits for 25 hours and 18 minutes, the first human to be in space for more than a day and the first to sleep while in outer space."

It reminded Lexi that even when part of your world ends the world at large progresses.

Lexi dug through the rest of the papers looking for the follow up. She found it and was devastated by the report. "The Sylvester family, consisting of a father and his two children, a 15-year-old daughter Ruby, and 10-year-old son

Derrick, were dropped on Admiralty Island for a lesson in survival, a hobby of Mr. Sylvester, when the sudden, devastating storm forced the charter plane scheduled to pick up the family, to abort the rescue.

"The storm claimed the lives of Mr. Sylvester and Derrick, though Ruby survived."

The article gave more detail about the boat the father and son had built out of logs that had tipped over during the storm. Ruby had been on shore and had taken shelter.

"A rescue helicopter picked up Ruby 18 hours after the storm began. The Coast Guard recovered the bodies of Mr. Sylvester and his son after the storm passed."

A third follow-up story included an interview with the teenage Ruby Sylvester. She was quoted as believing her family was abandoned by Fagan Charter. Ruby blamed Terry. Bob had said as much, but reading it sent a chill over Lexi. She started shaking as she sank to the floor clutching the newspaper.

Ruby was only 15 when she lost most of her family, the same age as Jada. At 23, Lexi was eight years older than Ruby was at the time her brother and father died. It was no wonder Ruby sounded bitter and vengeful in the article.

Lexi changed her mind. She definitely wanted to talk to Ruby Sylvester.

It was raining in earnest by the time she reached the top of the stairs and Lexi was drenched when she opened the door. She stripped off her raincoat and boots.

Kak and Doris sat at the kitchen table drinking weak sugary coffee. Doris called to her. "We're leaving in half an hour for the museum."

Lexi took a towel hanging in the hall and patted her hair. She walked into the living room, picked up the phone book, and called Ruby's number. She held her breath as it rang.

Ruby picked up the phone. Lexi found it hard to articulate who she was and what she wanted. Ruby seemed to have anticipated the call.

"I heard you were in town." Silence.

"I was hoping to meet you," Lexi stammered while nervously playing with the phone cord.

Ruby's response came quickly. "How about Monday?" That would be two days after July 4th. Lexi could hear Ruby flipping through a calendar. "Noon. You know where I live." She hung up.

Lexi was surprised by the "yes," but remembered Detective Reiger telling her that you should just ask the question. It was up to the person you asked if they wanted to answer, accept the invitation.

Stunned, Lexi hung up and wrote down the address next to the phone number in the phone book she had been staring at. She tore the scrap of paper off and stuffed it deep in her jeans pocket. She wanted to make sure Doris and Kak had not heard her conversation and poked her head around the corner into the kitchen. Doris was standing up and shoo-ing Kak out of the house.

"We need to get to the library." She said over her shoulder to Lexi.

"Gram," Lexi pleaded. "Do we have to go?" Doris practically pushed Kak into the front hallway.

"Put your boots on. Both of you."

8

While Lexi employs lessons she learned from Detective Robert Reiger, he is at home in Oakland discussing what he hopes is his last case with Jackie—only he's leaving out the biggest detail.

Robert and Jackie finished dinner. They cleared the dishes. He washed and rinsed and she dried and put away. They looked out the window into the backyard in silence. The young trees they had planted to replace a swing set cast long shadows as the sun faded.

"You made my favorite." Robert looked from the dish in his hand back to Jackie.

"Lasagna with meat sauce." This would be a night of discussion.

Reiger finished the last dish and handed it to Jackie. He moved behind her and put his arms around her waist. She smiled and rested her head on his chest. They stood for a moment, still and content.

Jackie shifted. "I'll make you some ice tea."

Robert kissed her and moved to the living room.

Once they had settled with their glasses, Jackie gave her husband a look that he recognized. She had something on her mind.

"I was talking to Principal Mathison today." She paused. They knew each other so well. They both knew what was coming. "She mentioned retirement."

"What was her tone?" He asked.

"Good." Jackie sipped her tea. "She wanted to remind me–and not for the first time–that I can retire with a full pension next year."

Robert smiled. "You put in your time."

"Loving it most of the time."

"Loving it." He repeated, waiting for her to say what she really wanted to say.

"I was thinking," Jackie looked at Robert, her dimpled cheeks deepening in a mischievous smile. "What if we both put in for retirement this year."

Robert said, amused. "You sound like Stryker."

"As if!" They laughed. This was a big ask and Jackie wanted to give her husband time to mull things over. She had talked about retirement for some time, but knew that Robert was not as open to it. She thought it was because he would not know what to do with himself. It was a concern of hers for him as well. She had been filling her summers with volunteering at church, a running club, and get-togethers with her teacher friends and family.

He felt a pang of guilt that he had not confided in her about his search for the driver. More like a dagger in his heart than a pang.

He drained his glass and set it down, collecting his thoughts.

"I do want to retire. It's probably past time, but I have one last case to solve."

Jackie knew what he was talking about. She searched his face, unsure what to say. Instead of speaking, she stood up and took their glasses to the kitchen and placed them in the sink.

Returning to the sofa, Jackie looked at her husband, a pained expression spread across his face. "If this is what you need to do."

"It is."

9

Lexi remembers the hours waiting for Doris at the library and museum more fondly than she expected.

Ketchikan had grown from a fishing village into a small town and the library also housed the tiny museum on Dock Street just up from the newspaper office. Once at the museum, which was two dimly lit rooms, Lexi trailed behind Doris and a small group of tourists from the cruise ship. It was as if she were a child again.

For years, after retiring from the phone company, Doris led bus tours. She and a handful of drivers would split up the sights, hitting the totem parks on either end of town, Saxman Village to the south and Totem Bight to the north.

There were plenty of damp caves to explore with fool's gold that delighted tourists even though the gold they could pick off the ground was worthless pyrite. The last place on the tour was the museum slash library. For the last 10 years, Doris could manage only the museum tour because her eyesight was not what it used to be.

Doris always took her docent duties very seriously, telling tourists that Alaska became a state in 1959, "but in 1867," Doris intoned as the general tourist population met her with eyes glazed over, "The United States paid $7.2 million to buy Alaska from Russia. It was handed over officially in October, 1867. Not too shabby. This area, the Tongass, was Russian territory and you can see Russian Orthodox churches if you visit Kenai and Sitka. We don't have one so don't go looking."

This lecture was the prelude to the most important talking points for Doris—those about the native artifacts portion of the museum. Doris wasn't the most patient of docents and bullied the tourists into reading the descriptions of the displays, which consisted of a few cases with antique button blankets, an eagle feather headdress which, as a teenager, struck Lexi as odd because she had never seen an ornate headdress like it at any native performance. There were also pieces of pottery, colorful trading beads, and cradleboards.

After an unsuspecting tourist from Wisconsin read "tingot" for "Tlingit" she corrected their pronunciation, "It's not 'tingot' it's 'CLINK-it' one of the tribes of Southeastern Alaska," she said before ringing the seaman's bell so loudly that everyone jumped.

Doris gave the same tour to all the tourists and, while she was rough with them, they loved her for it. In an impervious voice she would say, "And that" — she pointed to the word Haida —"is 'HIGH-dah.'" Doris waved like the Queen at the "HIGH."

Lexi smiled listening to Doris terrorize the crowd. It reminded her of the famous waiter, Ford Fong, at Sam Wo's in San Francisco's Chinatown where Lexi celebrated the holidays with her friends—the gang from the bakery, retired jazz singer Stella, the former private investigator, Henry, and the small in stature but large in personality Tiny Timm. Fong was notorious for abusing customers and ordering for them. It's why tourists flocked to the restaurant blushing and giggling their way through trying to order. Everyone liked having a good story to take home of Fong famously barking at them almost as much as their photos of the Golden Gate Bridge.

Inevitably, the one brave wise cracking tourist would joke that they had no idea there would be a test before they exited the library in a hurry. Before this moment arrived, Lexi peeled off to return a book Doris had borrowed. Her grandmother always wrote a review on the back of an old envelope leaving it in the book. Lexi read the envelope and chuckled.

Doris and the librarian were old friends. Sandra was like no librarian Lexi had ever met. In her early 70s, Sandra wore fish-net stockings, tight skirts, and cat-eye glasses that she used to peer across at googly eyed teenagers.

Sandra took the book and, winking at Lexi, tossed the envelope with the review into the trash can under her desk.

Lexi wanted to sit and think while she waited for Doris to wrap up her docent duties. The Sourdough Bar was a few blocks away on Front Street where Lexi could relax for the next half an hour.

10

Over beers at the Sourdough, Lexi discovers a secret about her mother and the answer to who "R" might be in June's diary.

In most small towns, there were more bars than churches and Ketchikan was no exception. The timber industry attracted a generation of young men to work in the 1960s and downtown had dozens of bars to show for it. There was the seediest, Shamrock, with nude dancing and brawls frequently reported in the crime blotter; local watering holes like the Sourdough and the Arctic offered a respectable environment with a little personality. Out at Thomas Basin harbor was the fisherman's bar, the Potlatch. There was a logger bar, the Totem. In a rare coming together of loggers and bush pilots, the Fo'scle, was a popular spot. And the Frontier Bar where the theater people performed "The Fish Pirate's Daughter" for tourists. Lexi was sad to see it had closed.

She recognized the bartender, Stevie, from school. They had not been friends but comfortably exchanged chit chat as Lexi nursed a beer.

Once Stevie busied herself with another customer, Lexi took the diary out of her book bag and started to read it in the dim light. Moments later, she felt a presence and looked up. The person standing near her was a sturdy middle aged woman, her gray hair pulled into a loose ponytail. Her heavily lined face broke into a smile when she saw Lexi.

She stuck out her hand. "I'm Rey Owens." Lexi shook her hand and introduced herself. Rey said, "Fagan, huh." Stevie approached, asking if Rey wanted her usual to which Rey nodded.

"You behave yourself, Rey," Stevie chided good-naturedly, setting the bottle and a glass on the bar. "You know I'm also the bouncer," said Stevie as she pulled up her shirt sleeve to show off a faded red heart tattoo on her bulging bicep, the word "Butch" written in the middle. This was a different Stevie than Lexi had known in high school.

"It's not even your season," Stevie said to Rey. Not waiting for an answer she left the bar to wait on a table of tourists.

"No," Rey said, turning to Lexi. "It's not the best month for whale watching." Rey motioned to the stool next to Lexi who nodded her ascent to sit. "Humpbacks move to warmer water in Mexico, Hawaii, and even Japan to calve in September. They don't head back until April and May." Rey threw a worn backpack onto the counter and sat down.

"How long of a migration is it?" Lexi was fascinated by the woman and the whales.

"6,000 miles round trip. It can take them up to eight weeks. The orcas stick around longer, of course. They follow the ice and the food to the Bering Straits. I see orcas even this time of year. You can see gray whales, the giant blues. I saw one that had to be 100 feet long once." She paused, giving Lexi the once over. "Whales always come back home but they have many homes." Lexi was perplexed at the intensity of the statement.

Rey patted the backpack. "These are my whale books." She reached inside and took out a slim volume and handed it to Lexi. "Whale Ways: Migration Patterns in the Alaskan Waterways."

She started to hand it back, but Rey waved her off. "It's yours."

Ignoring the glass, Rey took a swig of her beer from the bottle and looked Lexi in the eye. "You look just like her, June."

"You knew my mother?"

"Of course."

Lexi did not know what to say.

"No disrespect but none of us could figure out why she married your father. Especially after that Jim's Lake business. I know it happened before she met him, but everyone knew the story."

Lexi was embarrassed and blurted out the first thing that came to mind. "I've been learning more about my parents in the last 24 hours than I did during the 18 years I grew up here." She downed the rest of her beer and asked, "How did you know her?"

"June was doing a story on whale migration." Rey became animated. "I'd spotted a Baird's beaked pod, the giant bottlenose whales. Very rare. They like it cold and the water deep so this was something. You know, seeing them in the narrows. See, the beaked whales are known to be shy and smaller than most whales and are mistaken for freakishly large dolphins by people who don't know what to look for." She took a breath. "I mean, I say they are small whales but they still get up to 35, 40 feet. The females are even larger than the males."

Lexi shifted in her seat before asking. "And my mother?"

Rey's eyes drifted to a spot in the distance. "June. She was young, beautiful, and interested in everything. She should have stuck with journalism and stayed clear of Terry. It would have been us against the world."

Rey seemed to have forgotten she was talking about Lexi's father.

"Who is 'us'?" Lexi asked.

"Scientists." Rey snapped back to attention. "We were a tight group back in the day." Rey's voice trailed off. "We got to talking, your mother and I, about how the Bairds have teeth." She looked apologetically at Lexi. "It's hard for me to think of June." She was silent for a moment. "I loved your mother."

Lexi was floored. Did her mother have an affair with Rey? Was Rey the "RO" in the diary? She had a thousand questions but remembered what Reiger had told her and kept quiet as Rey collected her thoughts.

"June wasn't just beautiful to look at. She was beautiful on the inside. She was curious and funny and had the best laugh." Rey's voice drifted off. "She was dating Terry at the time. He was teaching her to fly. In the 60s, if a man thought a woman was smart or worth their time, they fell for them. I don't know. That's out of my field, but it was the only explanation I could come up with. He paid attention to her and encouraged her to fly so she married him."

Lexi had a feeling there was more to the story. She asked, "Were you and my mother 'close' close?" She did not know how to ask if they had been having an affair; it seemed preposterous.

"We were." Rey smiled. "She took me up to photograph the whales once. Just the two of us. We loved that old Beaver. We landed on Gravina and–" Rey looked away.

Lexi was speechless.

"It was so freaking cold." Rey laughed and shook her head as if coming back to the present. "That was the start."

Lexi was confused wondering the same thing Rey had all those years ago. Why had she married Terry? Lexi had done the math and thought that June had been pregnant with her at the time.

"I didn't know her." Lexi bit her lip to tamp down how much she missed her.

"I know." Rey said. "I'm sorry." She volunteered, "It lasted five months and four days. The day before she married Terry."

This was unexpected. Though hungry for stories about her mother and hating to change the topic, Lexi had to meet Doris in a few minutes. She wanted to know more about the Sylvesters and asked, "You know about Admiralty Island?"

"There might be something to the accusation that Terry didn't pick up that family on purpose. It was a bad storm, but you don't leave anyone stranded. He didn't seem to really try."

"I thought their deaths were ruled weather related."

"It was what was talked about at the time." Rey finished her beer. "I'm no expert. I was in the middle of my dissertation. I only came to town for the whales." She motioned for another beer before finishing her thought. "And your mother."

11

Her head full of the revelations about her parents, Lexi takes Ross up on his offer to play tour guide and visits the Potlatch Lodge for a traditional ceremony. She listens, reflects, and emerges from the cave-like lodge in love with a Raven.

Though the rain fell steadily outside, the lodge was dry. The tourists pressed against the wooden walls mesmerized by the steady drumming, the rhythmic chants, and the dancers as they turned into an eagle, frog, and bear in the center of the room. The familiar scent of damp smoke and cedar filled Lexi with sadness. The pull of her memories and the flood of insights into her parents were like pin pricks.

She was warned that her flawed parents might disappoint her, confuse her, even disgust her. And these were not memories, just stories.

Ross's grandfather, Charlie, spoke before the ceremony. "I'm going to talk about story." All eyes were on him. A low drumming filled the room.

"We are sitting in a cedar big house for Potlatch. It was not just a place to gather, it was a place to administer justice — the center of our legal system that ruled for thousands of years. This cedar big house, like the totem poles surrounding it, were restored by my ancestors."

The drums went silent. "When the white people came, they exposed us to disease that killed us, their contact destroyed our economy, we were attacked and will never forget Angoon." He looked around the crowded room. A single drum was joined by another, low and steady.

"We will never forget Kake. Trade between families and tribes ended and, in order to survive, we moved to the towns leaving the clan signatures, the totems, to rot in the forest. But–" Charlie paused dramatically as the audience collectively held their breath "— things are changing. We are using the oil money that's been coming in to revive our culture. It's a dance with the devil I suppose. This park is full of our culture." He took a deep breath.

His face darkened. "We borrow this earth from our children, that is our tradition." The tourists shifted in their seats.

"That's enough history for now." Charlie grinned. "You're off the hook." The room filled with nervous laughter.

Lexi looked at Ross as the drums and chanting rose. His face concentrated into a stern prayer, his body swaying with the other dancers as they circled the room stamping their feet with growing urgency. The ground shook as the drumming and singing grew louder.

In the wooden hall, many clans were represented. Thunderbird, dogfish, crow, frog, eagle. Lexi was hot and light headed. The raven dancer whirled around the room, a carved raven head bobbing, the black and red felt robe bouncing with each step of the dance. The mother-of-pearl buttons on the robe flashed in the low light. The Raven flew with every step. His sleek black hair braided down his back. Ross's face was serene as his voice rose and fell in meditative song; his voice, along with the others, telling the story of the earth, the sky, the sea, his ancestors, and the future.

The familiar scene from her childhood field trips to the lodge transformed into a ritual. The chanting filled her senses as the dancers let her see them. The drums let her feel them.

As the dance ended, the audience slowly came out of its trance, clapping and smiling. Ross came up to Lexi, leaned in, and kissed her on the cheek. Flushed, she beamed up at him. He told her he would find her after he changed and disappeared in the crowd of mingling tourists and dancers. Lexi thought she spotted Sister Bernadette across the room.

Once outside with Ross, Lexi felt the spell dissipate. She turned to look at the long house made of red cedar, the front carved. In the center of the building a totem pole reached for the sky. At its base was the oval opening they had just exited. She marveled at it as if seeing it for the first time.

Waking through the sparse forest of totem poles, Lexi took Ross's hand. He squeezed it in return and said, "I have heard from the elders that the totems come to life as they are carved. I felt it myself since my grandfather started teaching me last year."

"You weren't into this stuff as a kid. It's pretty exciting. What changed?"

"We were warriors, you know. It's a lot of work to reclaim our culture but this is the time. Just a few years ago I joined our Canadian brothers and sisters to stop old-growth cutting on Haida Gwaii. There were elders and children. It was—" Ross looked away.

"Do you think we want to perform for tourists? We do it because we are proud. We honor our ancestors with every step. It's communion. It shows that we are still here."

"So much has changed." Lexi rested her arm on Ross's shoulder.

"The difference is that the tourists come and go but we are still here. We never left." Though there was no recrimination in his voice, Lexi felt a sting at how she had left, with barely a backward glance.

He looked around the park, pointing to a totem with a sea monster. "All of these are thought to be in their afterlife."

Something about this statement struck Lexi. The afterlife. Was it the dead who were in an afterlife, or the living after someone they loved dies.

They saw Sister Bernadette standing with a group of older women who looked like tourists. Lexi and Ross waved to her and the Sister waved them over. Ross walked to the cluster of women, said hello and turned to Lexi. "I gotta run. See you around."

Lexi starred as Ross ran toward his friends emerging from the lodge. Sister Bernadette introduced her companions. "These are nuns from my old order." Lexi must have looked surprised because Sister Bernadette said, with a smile in her eyes, "Yes, we take vacations."

Lexi said, "I wouldn't expect to see you at a traditional dance." Sister Bernadette winked. "You shouldn't be surprised. I have lived on this island since I was your age. The place is Indian country. More ancient than Jesus by generations." Her eyes twinkled. "You see why they sent a young Sister Bernadette here? Those are not the kinds of ideas the church endorses. 'Send her to the last frontier' they said and here I am."

"Then why do you keep wearing the habit after Vatican 2? You don't have to." Lexi had wondered before but never felt comfortable asking until now.

"The outside is only the mantle. It's the inside where life takes place. God knows where my heart is. I wanted to forget the outside so I could work on my spiritual life. It's easier when you don't have to think about what you'll be wearing any given day."

The nuns tittered their approval like teenagers at the mall.

"Watching the dancers give spiritual thanks to nature brings me closer to God."

One of the women said, "We don't take vacations from God."

12

Lexi's investigation might be stalled with Doris insisting that the funeral, the Fourth of July Drum & Kazoo Parade, and the "celebration of life" at Kak's house will happen on the same day.

Lexi stared at a stack of albums leaning against the console in the living room. She pulled out The Irish Rovers, one of the only groups to tour Alaska. More power to them, Lexi thought. They had a captive and loyal audience.

She felt a tug on her head as a strand of hair was pulled from her head.

"Ouch!"

"Was that attached?" Doris asked as she disappeared into the kitchen.

"Yes." Lexi said, smoothing down her loose curls; though she had to smile with the familiarity of the scene. "Thanks for making me feel at home." She followed Doris into the kitchen.

"I have a new plan." Gram sounded triumphant. "On the 4th, we have a quick funeral in the morning, go to the Drum & Kazoo Parade after, and end up at Kak's for the wake."

"Gram, the funeral doesn't have to be on the 4th. What happened to 'we'll get everyone to Kak's at half past eleven?" Lexi whined. "Besides, shouldn't we skip the parade this year?" Doris filled a sauce pan with water using one hand and with the other, she took a dish towel and draped it over her shoulder. She stopped the faucet and looked at Lexi.

"Everyone will be in town for the parade so they can come to the funeral before. The wake at Kak's will be after the parade. I have it all worked out." Doris put the pan on the burner and patted Lexi's arm. "Besides, your grandfather loved the 4th of July. He was a true patriot." Doris pointed in the direction of the framed Purple Heart in the living room. "He never missed the parade so we're doing it for him. I dug your costume out. Not sure it'll fit. You put on a few pounds in San Francisco."

"Gram," Lexi pleaded, "It's the drum and kazoo parade with clowns and the First City Players goofing around. People can't come to St. Mary's wearing costumes."

"Of course they can. Brody would have loved that." Doris started the coffee before walking to the couch in the living room where she picked up a bag and handed it to Lexi. "Besides," Doris continued, "the veterans always march in their uniforms, except the ones who are in the play."

Lexi opened the bag and shook out the pink clown suit Doris had made for her when she was a teenager. Doris took the bag and hugged it to her like a doll.

"This is very patriotic." She said, sarcastic. "It's a clown."

Lexi pressed the costume to her body. "It'll never fit. I may not work at McCracken's anymore but I see my friends there on weekends. It's a good thing they don't have a bakery here. I didn't know what I was missing. Have you ever had a Russian teacake?"

"Who are those friends again?" Doris said absently.

"You remember. Henry, Tiny Timm, the little person on crutches? He always asks me to run away with him to "The Kasbah." And Stella?"

Doris stared blank, the empty bag sagging in her arms.

"I guess I remember. Wasn't there some accident or something? I told you it was dangerous in the lower 48s."

"This from a woman who carries a pistol to a poker game." Lexi spread the polkadot jumpsuit on the back of the couch and repeated, "It's never going to fit." She was relieved. "Besides, I am not wearing this. I'm a grown woman. Can't I attend the parade and not be in it for once?"

"I'll sew a piece in there. Expand it a bit."

"Let's skip the parade for once."

"Absolutely not. Just think how Brody would have laughed at the look on Father O'Malley's face when he looks into the pews."

Lexi was miserable.

"If you won't wear it," Doris sighed dramatically, "you won't wear it." She picked up the clown outfit and wrapped it carefully before putting it back in the bag.

Lexi relented. "Okay, if you want to fix it I'll wear it." Lexi hugged her grandmother. "I'll bring a dress for the funeral to change into after the parade."

Gram grinned, victorious.

13

Lexi catches up with her chum Carl over drinks at one of the dozens of bars in a town without a stop light. Initially awkward, things lighten up as they renew their friendship.

I t was a Friday night and, for Ketchikan, the streets were busy. "Serpentine Fire" by Earth, Wind & Fire played on the jukebox when Lexi walked into the Fo'scle to meet Carl, the one friend she had kept up with, though spotty and intermittent, since leaving town. The light was dim. Before her eyes adjusted, she could smell sawdust, stale smoke, and strong liquor. It was a bit of a thrill to be in a bar here. There were a handful of bars downtown and several at the edges of town that she thought of as adult places, full of secret, grown up things.

As the room came into focus, her absence from town, and her friends, was starting to feel like neglect. She had left right after high school, at 17. Other than the Frontier, where her grandparents worked the lights for a summer show, she had never set foot in the other bars.

Lexi stood in the entry looking lost. Carl walked in behind her. At first they looked at each other unsure of what to say or do. After an awkward moment Carl lifted Lexi off the ground as they screamed, delighted to see each other.

He still had his boyish good looks and tousled hair from when they were at White Cliff High.

Lexi sat in a booth at a table near the front and motioned for Carl to sit next to her, "I feel so grown-up meeting at bars and day drinking."

There was a whiff of awkwardness. "Welcome to life in Ketchikan after high school," he said.

"Why haven't you ever come to visit the gay mecca?"

"I mean–" Carl stammered. "I wanted to, but–"

She interrupted him, "You must come."

"Honey," Carl looked at her, serious as a heart attack. "It's not like I work on the pipeline. You know I work with my dad."

Lexi said, "Nepotism, anyone?" There was a pause when Lexi thought she had miscalculated and that the night was going to be one long miscommunication. The thought that they had lost their friendship was a blow.

After what seemed like a long time, they both started to laugh.

"I can't help it if my dad's the Mayor." They giggled like school kids, relaxing into an easy, familiar banter.

"We are so old," lamented Carl.

Lexi protested. "We're only 23!"

"Har har." He ran his hand through his hair. "Do you know how old that is in gay years?"

A waitress came to take their order looking bored as they discussed what to drink.

"Manhattans!" Carl lit a cigarette and waved it around in a dramatic arc. "Whiling away hours in a smoky bar drinking Manhattans."

The waitress rolled her eyes and disappeared, returning a short time later with their drinks.

"I love a good Manhattan." He took a sip. "There should be a drink named for every city, don't you think? Like the Long Island Ice Tea."

"The East Coast has all the names." Lexi chimed in. "How about 'The San Franciscan,' a vodka martini. Russian vodka, vermouth with a handful of berries pierced with a rainbow flag stir stick and a twist of lemon rind."

"Very twisted." He winked as they clinked glasses. "A dirty San Franciscan would be fruit juice in the glass." Carl smiled. "You're terrible at this game."

Carl and Lexi had bonded over being picked on at Holy Name by the older kids. She because she lived with her grandparents and her parents had died. Looking back, Lexi thought the kids that teased her must have been afraid that their own parents might die.

Carl's family was from the rich side of town, which was not saying much since it was only a block long. Carl was the youngest of six kids. There had been a rumor in grade school that Carl had webbed feet. Even as the sixth graders when he pulled off his socks to show that his toes were just like theirs, it never stopped them from teasing him.

"I'm sorry about Brody. How's Doris holding up?"

"She's better than I expected. She and Kak are going through his things pretty quickly." She took a drink of the water the waitress put in front of her. Lexi remembered the breakfast table from the other morning when Kak was over. "Some things haven't changed. Doris is still digesting a donut from 1972." They giggled.

Lexi said, "Now tell me about you."

"I have news since I last wrote you." Carl's cigarette ash was about to fall. He looked for an ashtray. Spying one on another table, he gently guided his cigarette to it.

Lexi followed Carl's ash with her eyes and applauded when he flicked it into the ashtray. He sat back down and said, "Remember Felix? Indian. Cute." Lexi's face was blank. "He moved here to live with his aunt when we were in high school? He was on the football team?" He didn't wait for her to respond. "He's my boyfriend."

Lexi was embarrassed she did not remember Felix. She said leaning into him, "Awe, the King Salmon mascot. You were so cute in your crown and fish tail!"

"Good 'ol Chinook Salmon. I had pink glitter and papier-mâché in every hole in my body. I was a royal pink mummy." Carl returned her friendly lean before continuing talking about Felix. "He moved here from Haines because his family's very religious. I think Haines has two churches and 10 people. It was cruel to move him in the middle of high school, but lucky for me. They really did a number on the natives. Imported a hatred of gays they never traditionally had. Did you know—" He stopped, giving Lexi the once over.

"This look is working. Jean skirt, Keds." He peered at her shirt. "Is that vintage?" He touched the nubby fabric of her sleeveless shell from the 1950s.

She grabbed a handful of peanuts and missed her mouth. Carl feigned disgust before picking up the scattered peanuts and eating them. The alcohol was going to their heads and Lexi was feeling expansive.

She tried to focus. "I have something to tell you."

Carl went silent.

"My mother was having an affair with a woman before she married my father."

"June!" He said excitedly. "We hardly knew ya!"

"Well I never knew her period." Lexi said in an attempt at gallows humor.

"This deserves a drink. Garcon!" Carl motioned for the waitress who was not amused.

"Another round s'il vous plait!"

The waitress rolled her eyes and walked toward the bar.

"I wonder what other secrets your mother kept?" He said before draining his glass.

Being with Carl again was like the best part of high school, really the only good part for Lexi.

Carl gave her a side hug. "I didn't even know how much I missed you."

"Me either." Lexi took hold of his hand and squeezed it as he released her. Carl gave her a serious look. "Didn't you have a crush on that native boy?"

Lexi squirmed.

"Ross! That's him, right?" Carl was talking so loudly that a few patrons at the bar turned around and stared at them. Lexi shushed him. He whispered, "Speaking of Ross, isn't that his auntie at the bar?"

Behind the bar, Lexi recognized Margaret, the airplane mechanic at Fagan Charter and her parents' friend. She and Carl waved. Margaret waved back.

He turned back to Lexi and said, "You still like him."

"Stop." Lexi protested. "It was a schoolgirl crush."

He said, "you have someone in San Francisco." Before Lexi could protest, Carl leaned closer and whispered, "A boy or a girl?"

"None." She fumbled over her words. "Neither. No one."

Carl ignored her. He was looking around the dimly lit room. "Who do we know and who do we want to know?" Carl gave a whimsical curl to his lips. They were both getting sloppy drunk.

"Is that why we met here at the Fo'scle?" Lexi gave him the side eye. "A logger bar so you can find some action?"

"Lumberjacks are my weakness," he said, sheepishly.

She gave him a stern look.

"I know." Carl said. "It hurts his feelings, but we have an open relationship."

He pointed to Margaret before continuing to glance around the room. "Darling, someone has already clocked me. You talk to Margaret and I will see you later." They stood at the same time. Carl headed to the men's room and Lexi to the bar.

14

Things are hopping at the Fo'scle. Margaret drops a bombshell about the Fagan plane crash.

Margaret looked the same every time Lexi had seen her: overalls embroidered with the imagery of eagles, ravens, bears, and beavers, a few patches covering holes. Her hair, long and sleek, flowed down her back, iridescent like raven feathers in the low light of the bar. Her skin was wrinkled and sun-brown. If she were around her mother's age, she would be in her early 50s. She was sitting at the bar nursing a drink. Her husband Johnny sat at the other end of the bar with a small group of men.

"Margaret Abrams." Trying to sound casual and not like she was about to interrogate her about the accident, Lexi said, "I've been meaning to talk to you. You don't mind if I–"

Margaret motioned to the seat next to her "What'r you drinkin'?" She spoke slowly, deliberately. Lexi recognized it as the unhurried and thoughtful way many native Alaskans spoke.

"I'd better switch to coffee." Lexi nodded to the bartender who had been listening while talking to another patron. He poured the coffee and set it in front of her.

"How long's it been–" Margaret paused. "–since you took up in the south?"

"About six years."

"Back for Brody's funeral?"

Lexi nodded. They sat in silence for a moment nursing their drinks when Margaret brightened and said, "I hear you've been hanging out with my nephew."

Lexi blushed and thought, *small towns.* "We have. I feel bad that we lost touch when I moved but when I saw him at Holy Name, it was like old times."

Margaret nodded. It felt familiar to Lexi. Margaret was someone who was always around, playing poker at her grandparents, working on cars and motorcycles at a shop off Front Street.

"I really like him," Lexi said tentatively thinking of how he ran off with his friends. "But I'm not sure how he feels about me." Lexi was sure she had made a mistake confiding in Ross's aunt. She didn't know Margaret that well. She was an adult in Lexi's childhood.

Margaret sat quiet for what felt like a long time. She put down her beer and looked directly at Lexi and said, "Indian men show their love through action. They may dance for you. Or build you something. If Ross brings you dried fish, he likes you." Margaret's eyes drifted down the bar to her husband. "That's how Johnny courted me. He brought me crabs from his boat and fixed the pilings on my house. I understand that kind of love."

Lexi said, "I think of myself as a woman of action."

Margaret's eyes turned to Lexi. She looked at her face, her crown of curls that had escaped from the knot. Margaret said, "Then be a woman of action."

Lexi smiled as if she had just received a gold star.

Margaret sighed, shifting the energy, and said, "I miss your mom."

"I think you must miss her more than me." Lexi realized how that might sound and said quickly, "Only because you knew her."

"Your mom was good people. She would fly medicine to remote villages for nothing. It was behind your dad's back. We would work out when your father was busy. It was very cloak and dagger."

Lexi could not have wished for better stories about her folks.

"I might miss the plane, the Little Blackbird, as much." Margaret took a swig of her beer and gave Lexi a wink.

"I didn't know the plane had a name."

"Of course." Margaret smiled. "Your mother named her. She was funny, your mom. It was a joke, really. The SR-71 Blackbird was a Mach 3 Lockheed reconnaissance plane—a spy plane. It was fast and could fly at great altitudes. Well, ours was a de Havilland DHC-2 Beaver, slow and noisy, but we loved her. It was the perfect bush plane, great for short take offs and landings on land or at sea. Single engine. Your mom named her because of that small plane used for spying and our old lumbering Beaver was—"

Lexi smiled and finished the sentence, "—The Little Blackbird." Talking about her parents was thrilling. There was so much she didn't know. Their lives were starting to form in her mind. Her mother's diary entries about how exciting it was to learn to fly. The image of her jumping in the Little Blackbird, checking the engine, taking off from the dock, landing on an air strip to drop supplies or pick up passengers.

Margaret sighed heavily. Her tone changed. "There is no way June and Terry just went down. I can fix any plane. The Beaver, it was a workhorse. Terry bought it off the military. They stopped making them in '67. There was nothing wrong with that plane. I kept it in top shape. Just that morning, I did a full check. All three fuel tanks were full. And your mom was a great bush pilot. You have to sense a storm is coming, gauge downdrafts and read the wind and turbulence so you can ride it. You have to be up here. The weather is fickle like a teenager. Sunny one minute then a Southeaster comes up like a temper tantrum."

Lexi was bewildered.

"There was an investigation."

Margaret shrugged. "Of course. They said it was an accident, but I don't buy it. There was no reason the plane would crash. I knew that plane inside and out. It was a dead calm day. It wasn't even raining. Why would the plane go down? As it happened, your mom ended up flying the plane. She was a better pilot than your dad."

Realizing what she had said, Margaret put her hand on Lexi's arm. "I'm sorry." Lexi gave her a reassuring smile. "This is a lot. I should let it go but–" she trailed off.

"I was always told they went down in a storm," Lexi paused to think about what she was hearing.

Margaret looked at Lexi with pity. "Hon, Doris and Brody told you that because there was no explanation. How could you have understood as a kid when no one understood it."

Lexi was trying to think through every scenario. "What do you think happened?"

"I just don't know." Margaret shook her head. "We did a lot of oil company business. They were our biggest clients at the beginning when they were figuring out the pipeline, where there was oil, if there was oil. Everyone racing to find it. Like everything up here that has to do with resources, it was the wild west. Maybe what Professor Parker did was a secret?"

"Who's Professor Parker?"

"Samantha Parker. Something fishy there." Margaret's voice dipped as if she did not want to be heard.

Lexi asked for details but Margaret waved her off. "Don't listen to me. I'm getting paranoid in my old age. Forget about it."

Lexi sipped her coffee. Questions zipped around her head, but she stayed quiet, hoping Margaret would keep talking.

After a bit, Margaret said, "Everything was secret in those days. Oil is the gold of the 20th century. Wouldn't want your competition to know where you were exploring. Not just that, not everyone was on board with it."

They stared at the rows of bottles behind the bar until Margaret shook her head. "I think it's been long enough. You need to hear the truth." She turned and looked Lexi in the eyes. "The Little Blackbird going down." She lowered her voice. "I've never thought it was an accident."

"What?" Lexi was floored. "Did you tell the police?"

Margaret shook her head. "I didn't want to draw attention to Johnny," she looked at her husband laughing with his friends down the bar.

"What does Johnny have to do with it?"

Margaret looked at Lexi for a long time before answering, "Okay. Buckle up. I'm going to tell you something that is not to be repeated. Promise me, Alexandra."

Lexi nodded.

"At that time," Margaret whispered, "and mind this is over 20 years ago, Johnny was drinkin' and he sometimes smuggled grass on charter planes when they were headed north to big towns, Juneau, Fairbanks, Anchorage. It was small stuff. When I found out I made him stop. You could be put away for a long time if they found even a little pot on you and dealing–forget it. I didn't trust the people he was hanging out with. They would have narked on him if they had been caught. It was dangerous."

"You didn't want the police to look at Johnny so you never told them there's no way the plane crashed?" Lexi was incredulous.

"I had no way of proving anything, but it never made sense. And–" She put her hand gently on Lexi's arm. "–he's a good man. He just lost his way. He'd been going to school, but his past caught up with him and he fell off the wagon." Margaret took a drink to steady herself.

Not thinking, Lexi asked, "Why are you still with him?"

Margaret straightened her shoulders and said, "Not that it's any of your business." Before Lexi could apologize, Margaret continued. "You know, I never know how to answer this question." She sighed. "Yes, I get it a lot."

Lexi held her gaze, she continued: "For me, it's always been love." That was not what Lexi expected to hear. "I always wanted kids and after six years together, I finally got pregnant and lost the baby." The words rushed out of her. "Johnny fell apart. I always knew he was still in there somewhere. My loving husband. He still is."

Lexi suddenly felt she needed to get away from this sadness. The revelation of what she had always known as an accident called into question made her want to cry and to scream. Margaret, someone Lexi had called "auntie" her whole life, had told her so much that she needed to process. To steady herself, Lexi looked for Carl, but he was nowhere in sight.

She looked back at Margaret.

"You need to know everything. Johnny had been taken away from his parents and put into a boarding school when he was a kid. They cut his hair and beat him when he spoke Tlingit. His pain is deep and I know he fights the drink as much as he can." She looked at Lexi, her face drawn. "No matter how far he falls, he always comes back to me." Margaret looked at Johnny. "He's a sensitive man."

Margaret said, "He needs to take the edge off life sometimes." It was obvious Margaret wanted to talk.

"How did you two get together?"

"This won't make sense to you but I believe in spirit. Johnny and my spirits are linked." Margaret's face lit up. Could this be Margaret? As she spoke, Lexi could picture what she was describing. A young woman full of love and hope. A young man struggling with a terrible childhood. The two of them catching a ferry out of Ketchikan. The town getting smaller as they turned their heads to the future.

Hitchhiking to San Francisco and Alcatraz, another island that became a symbol to the native people but this time not of what they had lost but what they would gain in recognition. She pictured Margaret's hair, long and sleek. Johnny wearing an old Army jacket snug over his slim frame. Purpose was their bond. Native pride their glue. That was before alcohol gripped him, had wounded them, but, looking at Margaret's face as she told the story, it had not destroyed them.

There was a commotion at the other end of the bar. Johnny patted his buddies on the back, waved to Margaret and Lexi, and walked outside.

"In those days, Johnny was hanging with bad people. Alaska is a place a lot of people come to escape their lives, to hide. Some'r running from the law, they come here because they don't wanna be found."

Lexi had moved to San Francisco to find out who she was outside the microscope of her small town; it had never occurred to her that Alaska was a destination. A place to run to.

"Why are you telling me this?"

"Because I want you to see Johnny how I see him." Margaret smoothed her hair. "He was having a hard time. He was promised a job on the pipeline if he just did a few little jobs for them. But, he did not cause the crash."

"Finding out about what Johnny was doing must have been hard on you."

"It was hard on him." There was longing in Margaret's voice as she put her head in her hands.

Lexi gave her a moment to come back to herself before she asked: "Do you think the plane was sabotaged because of the drugs, even if it wasn't Johnny who did it?"

"Of course not. But that doesn't mean the pigs wouldn't think that. I didn't have any evidence somebody tinkered with the plane. It's just my gut. I had done a full check in the morning because Terry had a run in the afternoon. One thing that haunts me, though." Margaret took a deep breath. "June wasn't supposed to be on the flight."

Lexi wanted to ask questions, but stuck to the rule: sometimes it's best to stay silent and listen.

As if to confirm her instinct, Margaret continued. "They didn't often fly together. She worked at the paper to make ends meet. I suppose she flew that day because Terry wanted her company."

She looked toward the door where Johnny had just left. "And she wanted to fly, only he was always the pilot." Margaret drained her beer. The bartender lifted a fresh bottle, but she shook her head no.

"There's something else you should know."

Lexi held her breath.

"Bob and I have been piecing together the Little Blackbird as salvage appears over the last 20 years. We started with the only thing recovered just after the crash, the tail. Every time there's a storm, another piece of that plane seems to wash ashore someplace. If a fisherman or crabber sees anything, they radio in and I have one of my cousins bring it in."

Lexi was confused. "I understand why you want to figure out what happened, but why include Bob?"

"It's the story, innit. If I can discover why the plane went down he would have a hell of a story. Besides, he and your mom were close. She was a good reporter. He wanted her to quit the charter service and work full time at the paper."

Margaret seemed to run out of steam. She shook her head wearily and patted Lexi on the arm as if to dismiss her.

Lexi gave her a quick hug and left.

Outside the bar, Lexi saw Johnny smoking a joint. He looked sheepish. "It's just skunk weed. I don't do anything hard. Please don't tell Margaret."

"Do you think she doesn't know?" she asked.

Johnny's eyes implored her and she reassured him. "I won't say anything."

Johnny spoke loudly trying to articulate a thought but the words slipped away. "I just– you see–" He tried again. "She doesn't want to know." His blurry eyes broke contact with hers and he looked down at the wooden sidewalk covered with wet sawdust.

She did not know what to say.

Johnny looked from the ground back to Lexi. "Do you really want to dredge all this up? When you ask questions, the answers can hurt other people. I know what that's like. They took everything from me. I lost my language. I lost myself. Questions were beaten out of us. But you ask me anything, little Lexi. If it will stop you from bringing this up for Margaret's sake."

Lexi thought how each wanted to save the other from pain. She had always liked Johnny and, wanting to reassure him, she asked, "What is gumboot?"

Johnny burst out laughing.

Lexi had to get into her mother's diary to look for any reference to their clients: big oil or Samantha Parker, more on "R" who was probably Rey. She had not found any reference to the Sylvesters but, now that Margaret admitted she suspected the crash was no accident, Lexi needed to look again with fresh eyes.

15

Lexi confronts Bob after Margaret spills the beans about collecting salvage and trying to find a cause of the accident.

On her way home from the bar, Lexi stopped by the newspaper. She sat opposite Bob, who was leaning back in his chair with a pencil in his hand.

She came to ask him about the plane's wreckage but he had started talking about his current opinion piece on why people moved to Alaska so she let him talk.

"Number one," Bob said with a wink, "Hippies come for the back-to-nature stuff. Then, there are the start overs. I know a guy who ran away from a car payment. Can you imagine?" His chair was dangerously close to tipping backwards. "There's the last chancers. Years ago, a guy from Michigan was frustrated with his wife. She'd raised the kids and, after they left for college, she was floundering around driving him nuts so he sends his wife's resume off without her knowing and she gets the job! They up and moved. She's now the principal of Kayhi."

"Mrs. Dunnigan!" Lexi giggled. "White Cliff's Mrs. Dunnigan."

Bob set his chair down with a thud. "Listen, I gotta get back to work." Lexi leaned forward, she needed to ask Bob the question she had come to ask, "How come you didn't tell me you and Margaret have been looking into the plane crash?"

Bob's energy dropped. "At first I thought she was onto something, but it's been 20 years. Margaret has collected a lot of the plane."

"She told me."

"It's stored out at the old hangar."

Before Lexi could ask one of the many questions swirling in her head, he said, "After all these years, we've reached one dead end after another." Bob took a deep breath and ran his hands through his hair. "Listen, I don't want to dismiss Margaret like that. You should talk with Professor Sam Parker. She can tell you more about your folks. That's really what you're after. To know them, right?"

"Yeah." Lexi admitted. "Which oil company did Professor Parker work for?" He looked surprised that she knew about Parker.

"Something's been bothering me," she continued. The pipeline is a thousand miles away in Prudhoe Bay, what did anyone here have to do with it?"

"It was like the gold rush days. Everyone wanted a piece of the pie. Big oil was doing environmental studies all over the state to make it look like they cared. There was a lot of money flowing up here. Sam's a local. This was her base. She liked flying around feeling like a big shot telling people she was working for some non-affiliated environmental group but it was your mother who figured out the professor was working for big oil. June knew that where Parker was flying was nowhere near the pipeline because it was Fagan Charter Parker used for transportation."

Just then the phone rang. Bob answered and started scribbling some notes on a notepad. He covered the receiver and said to Lexi, "The non-profit was a shill for North Sea Oil but I think Parker was moonlighting for all of 'em."

Bob listened to the person on the other end of the line for a minute while jotting down notes. He hung up and said, "I gotta go. Theft at the museum.

Probably a kid's prank." He ran toward the door. "You can find Parker in the phone book."

The door closed behind him leaving Lexi alone.

As long as Lexi had the office to herself, she decided to do some digging. She went down the hall to the room with the old filing cabinets, located a file on the pipeline, and worked backward to find information from before the pipeline had been built. She found a few articles on the competition for the oil contract. One mentioned Professor Samantha Parker conducting environmental studies. She made a photocopy of the article that had a photograph of the professor, a young woman who looked like a college student.

At the bottom of the file drawer, in between folders, was a slip of paper. She dug it out. It was a check for $5,000 made out to Bob from the North Sea Oil Company. She knew there would be a logical explanation and put it in her pocket to ask him about the next time she saw him.

The day's information made her feel giddy with knowledge. She needed a way to organize the material but had no clue where to start. On the off-chance she could reach Professor Parker, she looked her up in the phone book and dialed the number from Bob's office.

Parker answered the phone and, to Lexi's surprise, was eager to meet. She was free now for lunch.

There were only a few restaurants in town. The Elks Club that Brody had been a member of since the beginning of time, and a Chinese restaurant on Creek Street that had been open since the Gold Rush. Since the bars served food, they decided to meet at the Pioneer Bar.

Lexi was seated at a table among the tourists when a tall, middle aged woman arrived. Waving her over, Lexi noticed the professor's pants were workmen-like and her shoes sturdy, but her blouse was billowy, her white hair piled on top of her head in a neat bun with loose pieces framing her face.

As she sat down, Parker pushed her bangs from her eyes. It was an incongruous package: rugged from the waist down and feminine from the waist up. She noticed Lexi watching her and smiled revealing perfect white teeth. She said, "Everyone underestimates me because they don't know what to make of me." Lexi laughed.

The waitress appeared and took their order. Lexi needed food. She ordered a sandwich and a Coke. Parker ordered the same. They sat in awkward silence until the sodas arrived. Taking a drink, Lexi asked, "What do you mean 'everyone underestimates you?'"

"I'm a woman who works in the oil business. And I just happen to be gay."

Lexi quickly re-evaluated Professor Parker. There were no "P" or "S" initials in her mother's diary.

"Bob Kinkaid, at the paper, told me that you worked for the oil companies but hid your connection to them."

Parker belly laughed, putting her hand on her stomach. When she caught her breath she said, "Bob, through June because she flew me around, was always trying to connect me to big oil. He finally busted me with a canceled check from North Sea Oil"

Lexi made a mental note that it had been her mother who had made the connection.

"How did he do it?" Lexi asked.

"He dug up a canceled check from the oil company. He got it from a friend at the bank so he couldn't print the accusations but I had to stop or compromise my position at the college."

Lexi wasn't buying it. "It was that easy to stop?"

"It was." Professor Parker said sheepishly. "That kind of money touches everything including higher education. They were pouring money into institutions. I would benefit legally so why take a backhander?" She had regained her footing. "Bob doesn't have clean hands. Everyone benefited from that kind of money rolling into town."

Lexi didn't trust her. Besides, this information did not lead anywhere nearer to what happened to her parents plane. She thought the Professor was trying to point the finger at Bob. Best to keep things murky to protect herself.

16

With trepidation and excitement Lexi sees her school friends, happy for the break from revelations about her parents.

Lexi walked up the stairs next to the newspaper office toward home. Her hands were still coated with newspaper ink and she was a little tipsy from the drinks she ended up having with Professor Parker. She was sweating. Strands of her hair were curling in her face and eyes. She scooped it back, smudging ink on her forehead and cheeks.

Near the top of the stairs, she saw Ross's sister Dot and their cousin Collette leaving the Old Hospital. When they spotted Lexi, they ran to embrace her.

Collette looked Lexi up and down. "You've changed."

Lexi felt shy. "I don't look that different."

Dot said, "It's your face." Stunned at first, Lexi looked at her hands and realized her face must have been smudged with newspaper. She let out a quick snort of laughter. It was as if no time had passed as Dot and Collette rubbed the ink off Lexi's face.

Dot lived in a house within walking distance and Collette and her family lived in the Old Hospital. Collette invited Lexi to say hello to her parents, to which Lexi happily agreed. Despite the appearance of the dilapidated hospital, now occupied by mostly native families, Lexi had spent many happy times playing in the halls, rummaging through the old chapel and abandoned operating rooms with Collette, Dot and occasionally Ross.

Collette went to public school, not Holy Name with Dot and Lexi, but after school and on weekends there was a lot to explore between the abandoned school near Lexi's house — empty classrooms and rafters were the perfect place to pretend to smoke cigarettes. Dot and Lexi took turns stealing Marlboros from Dot's uncle or sometimes a pipe from Lexi's grandfather. It was more fun to pretend to smoke a pipe and act and talk "old timey" than to choke on an actual cigarette.

As they walked into the Old Hospital, Collette told Lexi that she joined the police force right out of school.

The three walked down the musty hall that smelled of mold and wet plaster. First Dot, then Collette and Lexi, started running like when they were kids. The end of the hall was really the front of the hospital that no one used. The elevators were to the left, but no one remembered them working. They climbed the stairs, two at a time, to the top floor where Collette's family lived.

The Native kids in Lexi's circle were sometimes reserved with non-family and especially with non-Natives. It took some time to earn their trust. Dot did not warm to Lexi until the end of first grade. Lexi started visiting their home for dinners, eating chicken with rice and soy sauce, topped with seaweed strips Dot's mother dried on the front porch of their home not far from Lexi's.

Lexi felt proud to be accepted by some of the Native families of her friends.

Inside the make-shift apartment was a small, neat room with a hot plate where a large pot was simmering in a corner kitchen area. A bookshelf separated the kitchen from the living room.

There was a sagging couch and a barcalounger facing a rabbit-eared television behind a coffee table stacked with old magazines and more books.

Mrs. Kitwanga was stirring the pot. She looked the same as when they were kids except for two large white streaks at her temples setting off her black hair. She spied Lexi and threw her hands up. "Well, look what the cat dragged in!" Her warm welcome nearly made Lexi cry as she accepted the hug with gratitude.

Colette's mother had always been kind to Lexi. Mrs. Kitwanga motioned for Lexi to sit down. She told Lexi a story about her mother. Lexi had heard the story at the bar but coming from Mrs. Kitwanga meant a lot. While flying for other clients, June would drop medicine to her relatives in remote areas of Alaska. "I admired your mother. It was hard going sometimes. The weather wasn't always good and she couldn't always land so she circled until she could push the box out the window. She was a brave pilot. When we offered to pay her, she wouldn't hear of it."

Lexi was silent, not knowing what to say but wondering if her mother had been flying the plane, maybe they would have survived.

Mrs. Kitwanga seemed to sense Lexi's feelings and said, "I was sorry to hear about Brody. When is the funeral?"

"You know Doris. She wants it to be on the 4th before the parade."

Mrs. Kitwanga frowned. Lexi knew it was not how their family would honor their dead. She stood and returned to the pot bubbling on the hot plate.

"I'm making gumboot." There was a twinkle in her eye. Mrs. Kitwanga knew Lexi did not like the chito—a sea mollusc the three girls often collected in tide pools when they were kids to bring to Mrs. Kitwanga for dinner. Lexi would eat it with mounds of rice drowning in soy sauce to mask the briny flavor and the texture she imagined to be that of an actual boot. The girls dissolved in peals of laughter.

"Thank you but I have to get home. Doris is waiting for me." She hugged everyone goodbye.

"Don't make yourself a stranger," said Dot as Lexi turned to leave.

17

Lexi reconnects with her old pal Detective Reiger who, despite misgivings, gives her advice on how to investigate a crime.

The next morning, Lexi snuck out of the house early to make a call from the Mayor's office using the bat phone. Carl told her that, because Alaska had so much territory to cover, the Air Force had strung phone lines and left a phone in the Mayor's office that somehow remained unconnected to Ma Bell resulting in free calls. He told Lexi to come on the weekend or between 5pm and 6pm when everyone had gone home but the office remained open. It was a weekday but Lexi hoped she could find the office with the phone based on Carl's drunken description without being seen. Ketchikan City Hall, even on its busiest day, was like a mausoleum.

The main office was empty but she could hear someone down the hall making copies. At the other end of the hall from the Mayor's office, Lexi found what looked like the door Carl described. There was a notch near the lock. She tried the handle, unlocked. She ducked in and closed the door behind her. It was a spare, small room. The dark wood paneling gave the impression of a large closet. The only furniture was a desk with the black phone. She dialed Detective Reiger's number.

He answered.

"Detective, this is Lexi Fagan."

"The girl who can't stay out of trouble."

"That's me." She sat on the edge of the desk. "I'm calling from Alaska."

"You don't say." Reiger tried not to be impressed.

She wanted advice on the various threads that were unspooling, it seemed, with every conversation since she landed back in Alaska. Ruby Sylvester, Professor Samantha Parker, Johnny and the smuggled drugs, Margaret telling her the crash was no accident, a mysterious "R" in her mother's diary, but before diving in, she asked him how things were. He told her that his best forensics person, Linda, was transferred to another team giving Reiger fewer resources than other detectives.

"He's up to his old tricks then? What's his name? It's something funny."

"Sergeant Stryker," Reiger's voice went flat. "With a world-class chip on his shoulder. Present and accounted for."

She was upset at the sabotage, but also glad he was telling her about it. Reiger never said much about his work. Jackie and Robert were private people and Lexi was grateful when either of them confided in her.

It didn't matter how good a detective he was, everything he did seemed to irritate his boss. Detective Reiger had been in charge of the two cases Lexi got herself tangled up in. One case involved her new boyfriend at the time, and the other case, her boss. Through the unlikely coincidence that Lexi lost her parents and Detective Reiger and his wife had lost their teenage daughter, a friendship and trust had grown between the two that lasted beyond the cases.

"That's so unfair. Why do you stay?" Lexi asked.

"You sound like Jackie," Reiger chuckled. "I lost friends when I became a cop. But I knew that if I could find one criminal who hit someone walking to work or on their way to school"– his voice was low, controlled–"it would be worth it." She knew he was talking about his daughter.

Lexi stayed quiet. He continued. "And I did."

Lexi stood up and nearly dropped the phone. "You found the person that hit Jada?"

"I can't talk about it. I promise when I know more I'll fill you in." Reiger returned to the previous subject of his boss as if he had not just dropped a bombshell.

"Besides, I didn't work this hard to quit. Stryker is not going to win. You'll appreciate this. There's a push to hire more Black cops so they put my face on the billboards." He laughed.

"I bet that makes Styker happy."

"Delighted." Reiger looked at the clock. "Enough about work, let's get to why you called. We'd better keep this short. It's going to cost you a month's salary."

"That's the interesting thing. This call is free."

There was silence on the line.

"I think this is the first time I've stumped you, Detective Reiger," Lexi said with a laugh. "It's something to do with Alaska Telecom." There was still silence from Reiger so Lexi continued. "The Mayor's son told me about it—"

Reiger had heard enough. "Okay, but it doesn't answer how you're making a call from what sounds like an official line."

"Because I'm calling from the Mayor's office."

Detective Reiger said, "I don't want to know, do I?"

Lexi laughed. "Not really."

Reiger smiled, turning back to the subject at hand. "What can I do you for?" As the sun rose, Reiger's office had gotten hotter. He leaned back in his chair and loosened his tie.

"I'm in Ketchikan for my grandfather's funeral. You remember my mom's parents raised me after my folks died."

"Yes." He sat up. "My condolences to you and your family. Brody, right?"

"Yes, thank you." She was continually impressed with his memory. She took a deep breath. "I was talking to the mechanic who worked for my folks and she said she's sure the crash wasn't an accident."

"Lexi–" Reiger started to talk but Lexi cut him off. She knew he was going to say that when people die in accidents and loved ones can't wrap their heads around it, they will fill in any inconsistencies with conspiracies. They want a cause of death that is not an accident.

"I know what you're thinking." Lexi was talking fast. "That I see murder everywhere, but hear me out. You know I have my head screwed on right. There's something here. My parents' best friend Margaret was also their mechanic. Her husband, Johnny, was smuggling drugs on the plane. And the daughter of a family that died when my dad couldn't pick them up because of a storm still holds a grudge against him and she became a pilot. She'd know about planes."

"There is a difference between gossip and evidence."

"I know." She felt defeated.

Reiger looked out the window. The dusty metal blinds were open, letting in the light. He knew that Lexi would play this out with or without his help.

"Okay," he sighed, resigned. "Remember, your brain is trying to find a pattern but that can be a dead end and lead to confirmation bias. Don't fill in the blanks. If you are going to ask questions, you don't want to put words in people's mouths. Know what I mean?"

"I do."

Reiger said, "Be careful. You're uncovering secrets that have been buried for a reason. Things that might not have anything to do with your parents dying."

Lexi said with genuine gratitude, "I am listening."

"Life doesn't have a solution, Lexi. You will figure it out as you go."

Lexi could tell that he was worried that she might blunder around rattling cages. "If there is a killer," Reiger parsed his words. There was a familiar protective tone to his voice. "And that's a big 'if,' you be careful."

"You are sounding like my grandparents." Lexi caught herself. "Well, Doris, now."

Reiger thought before he spoke. "Your grandparents were caring for you the only way they knew how. And when you got older, they never thought of you as anything but a child."

Lexi was unable to speak for fear of crying.

"I don't want you to feel dismissed," Reiger said, confirming Lexi's suspicions. But I need to warn you. You might not like what you find when you dig things up. You told me no one ever talked about your parents. You're eager to fill in those blanks, but not everything leads to murder."

Lexi was losing the thread. She wasn't convincing him that there was something to explore.

"I know." Lexi stared at the phone. "If I promise to check in with you so I keep my head, will you help me?"

Reiger knew she wasn't going to be talked out of it. "What do you need to know?"

"How do I tell if someone is lying."

"Let's back up. If you're going to investigate, do it right. You need to set up a timeline of the day of the accident. People your parents came in contact with. Even friends. People who had access to the plane. Then make a list of who had a grudge against your parents and start a murder board." Reiger paused. "You aren't even going to ask me what a murder board is?"

Lexi laughed. "I know you're going to tell me."

"When you have a murder, or in this case a suspected murder, you need to organize the evidence. Try and find a picture of the suspects, if you don't have one, just write their name on a white board or tack paper on a cork board. Write the suspect's name and what evidence you might have. Evidence. Not suspicions. The timeline is what it sounds like. Work backward from the time the plane went down. Read newspaper articles about the accident. Find the police report or the equivalent. Maybe the Coast Guard wrote a report. Backtrack. Talk to anyone who was at the hangar when the plane took off. Record all of it on the timeline along with possible motives. Revenge. Money. Jealousy. A crime of passion."

"My friend Collette is a cop." Lexi felt a tingle of excitement. "I can ask her for the report. I'm sure she has friends in the Coast Guard."

"Now you're thinking." Reiger relaxed. Maybe Lexi would be okay after all.

Lexi gave him a run down of what she learned so far.

"Sounds as if this daughter—"

"—Ruby Sylvester."

"She has motive and knowledge of planes," Reiger continued, "but now you need to find opportunity. What was she doing during the time just before your parents boarded that plane? Could she have sabotaged it? And what would sabotage look like? How would she do it?"

"How do I find out?"

"Ask her."

"What if she lies to me?"

"Corroborating statements is part of it. Find someone who can verify what she tells you. If they say she was somewhere else, confront her, but, Lexi, be very careful. I know you can take care of yourself, but still." Reiger looked at his watch. He couldn't get used to a free long-distance call.

"It's the best way to keep track of possible suspects and to eliminate them after you've checked out their alibi. Now this is an old case so people's memories will be fuzzy. Promise me you won't be alone when you talk to Ms. Sylvester." Reiger sounded serious. "Asking questions will freak people out, even if they are innocent. Promise me you won't do anything silly."

"I promise."

"Mind you do." With that, Reiger rang off.

Lexi thought she heard someone in the hall and she put the receiver down gently, moving to the door. She cracked it open and saw a figure in the hall.

It was Carl.

"You scared me," she said. "I thought you were your dad."

"He's still at the Elks Club having breakfast." Lexi closed the door behind her and joined him in the hall. Carl continued, "What did we learn?"

"Timeline." Lexi and Carl linked arms and walked fast out of the building before anyone spotted them.

"And Murder Board."

They made plans to meet later at Carl's apartment. "The Rouge Arms," as Carl called the pink building he shared with Felix because "Pepto Bismol Apartments" did not pass muster. "Darling," Carl had told Lexi, "The pink building is way too on the nose."

Lexi left Carl at the bottom of the stairs. As she started climbing the stairs toward home, her excitement at telling Carl about her conversation with Reiger was wearing off. She felt in over her head. Investigating her parents deaths? Suspecting her parents' friends? What had she been thinking?

She walked into her childhood home sweating and out of breath as the phone was ringing.

"Gram?" Lexi called out, kicking off her boots. She walked down the hall to see Gram putting together a puzzle at the kitchen table. She turned on the light. Gram looked up, startled. Even though it was almost afternoon, the kitchen was dark as heavy rain clouds outside threatened.

"Can't you hear the phone? Why are you sitting in the dark?"

It was becoming clear that her grandmother was in need of more care than she had realized, or had wanted to acknowledge. Lexi walked into the living room and picked up the phone.

"Barnes' residence." It was Kak confirming their poker night that night. Lexi hung up and joined Doris at the table.

"Where've you been, dear?"

Lexi told her half the story, leaving out the information about Admiralty Island. "I saw Margaret," she said helpfully.

"She's a good egg." Gram lit up. "Thick as thieves she and your mom were. They didn't need your father most of the time."

Doris gave Lexi the side eye and waited for her reaction but it was exactly the kind of information Lexi was thirsty to hear. She was trying to play it cool but her face was bright and eager. "What do you mean?"

"Your dad, bless him, was a man who took the most difficult path. We called him 'hard way Fagan.' If there was a complicated way to do something, that was his way."

Lexi asked for an example. "If he was going hiking on Deer Mountain, he'd go off the trail." Gram's shoulders rose to her ears. "Why? Did he *want* to run into a bear?" Lexi had never seen this side of Doris before. It felt as if she were hearing things Doris had buried for a long time.

"What else can you tell me about them?" Lexi asked. "Or is there anything about the accident you can tell me?" This may have pushed it too far.

"Margaret's up to something." Lexi kept quiet hoping Doris would tell her what the "something" was, but no. "She's coming tonight."

"I'm seeing Carl and Felix tonight."

"It's an early game. You can go after."

Doris stood. "Now let's stop talking about it. Come to poker tonight."

This was how Doris always ended conversations about June and Terry.

After a four o'clock dinner, people started arriving for the game. Margaret, Kak, and Bob. Lexi knew that Doris had a pistol sitting on a doily in the drawer of a small table next to the front window. The one with the statue of a shepherdess holding a staff with a lone sheep standing at her feet. Lexi hoped it would stay in the drawer during the game.

As people arrived, Doris reminded them of the schedule for the next day. A short morning funeral, eight to nine, then the parade started at ten and Kak's after for the wake. She finished with, "Costumes are mandatory."

Everyone laughed thinking Doris was joking.

Margaret sat down. "I won't be at the parade. Whose independence would I be celebrating?" Everyone nodded. There were few Indians who celebrated Thanksgiving and the 4th of July. There was only one Native veteran Lexi could remember that walked in the parade when she was little. Her friends always came. The city's parade was less about patriotism and more about having a good time celebrating summer.

"It's a good thing the 4th lands on a Saturday," said Bob, taking a drink of his beer. "It's a ridiculously packed day. You could have at least spread it out over a few days so I could have something to write about on Sunday and Monday."

They played a few hands. Margaret was winning the penny kitty. The stakes were low but emotions ran high. The rain started to clear and, as if on cue, a group of ravens started pecking at the window and cawing loudly. Doris set her cards facedown with care, stood slowly and walked to the table with the Shepherdess statue and opened the drawer.

Everyone rested their cards against their chests and watched as Doris picked up the gun and walked to the sliding glass door to the deck and opened it. She walked outside and waved the gun near the birds as they scattered, cawing in protest. Lexi had only seen her Grandmother shoot the gun once during Doris' drinking days.

Lexi thought about when she was a little girl watching and listening to poker games from the stairs in her PJs. These were not early games but late at night games when there had been a lot of drinking involved. When the birds came, everyone put their cards down and pounded the table egging Doris on. Poker nights were not fun when she was a kid, but now that she had some perspective and appreciated that Ketchikan was a gold rush town that attracted a certain kind of boundary pushing personality, she could see that it was all in good fun. Besides, Doris did not shoot at the birds, just scared them with a shot into the air.

Lexi remembered Brody saying, "Love, bullets come down you know."

Doris closed the sliding door letting cold damp air follow her inside.

"You are a cruel and unusual guttersnipe," said Kak, testy because she was losing.

"Stop using three dollar words," Doris shot back. If she didn't know better, Lexi would think they were having an argument.

18

At the funeral–whether wearing costumes for the Drum & Kazoo Parade or in somber black–everyone behaved as Lexi expected.

It was morning, at least morning for Lexi. Doris would have been up for hours and on her second or third cup of weak coffee. Wrapped in a blanket, Lexi walked downstairs to the kitchen.

"Any chance of an eggnog breakfast?" she asked. Doris sat at the kitchen table flipping through the Ketchikan Daily News, a few pages of news compared to the thick San Francisco Chronicle Lexi was now used to.

"You're a big girl. There's eggs and milk in the fridge. Vanilla and sugar in the cupboard."

Something Lexi had yearned for had happened. She was no longer a child, yet, somehow, it wasn't as satisfying as she had imagined.

Doris said, "I never liked Terry but if I was gonna kill him, I'd have just shot him." Lexi looked at the drawer. "You would have shot my father with your raven gun?"

"Bullets land where they land," she said.

"That's not still loaded from last night?"

"What good is it if it's not loaded? I'm not going to bash someone over the head with it."

Lexi smiled and drank her coffee. At least Doris couldn't get into too much trouble up here. She was surprised at the threat to her father, but she knew if she asked for clarification she would get nowhere.

After making her own eggnog breakfast, Lexi put on the black dress she bought at the second hand store on Polk Street near her apartment in San Francisco and came downstairs to pack her clown suit.

"Listen to this," Doris yelled, shaking the paper for emphasis. "Here's an obit that says '101 year old Randy Newcastle died unexpectedly.'" They laughed. "Of course that Randy would try and upstage your grandfather by dying now."

Lexi said, "Gram, where are your hearing aids?"

"My what?"

"Hearing aids."

Doris continued to drink her coffee while reading the paper. Lexi knew this trick. She sat next to her, touched her arm and said, "Your ear bobs. Please wear them today." Doris grimaced and shrugged, a sure sign that she might or might not wear them.

Half an hour later, they sat on the bench near the front door pulling on their rain boots. It was muggy, which meant mosquitos.

"You smell like chemicals." Doris said, her voice losing its usual fire, Lexi knew it was in anticipation of the day they said goodbye to Brody.

"Eau de DEET," Lexi said, giving Doris a side hug. It was going to be a long day.

At the funeral at St. Mary's, the verdict, unfortunate to Lexi's way of thinking, was no hearing aids. Lexi knew this was the only way Doris was going to get through it. She needed a break from her grief. A joke between them that would ease her into losing the man she had spent most of her life with.

"Grandma, why are you wearing a black armband?"

"This is not for Brody," she said loudly even though she was leaning close to Lexi in the front pew.

"I'm mourning the death of my sense of humor."
Timid laughter came from behind them. It was a
joke Brody would have appreciated, Lexi thought.

Looking over her shoulder, Lexi saw Ross at
the back of the church. She waved at him and he
waved back.

Kak wore a purple jumpsuit and a large black
hat walked down the aisle like the Queen Mother
nodding to mourners sitting in the pews. Everyone
craned their necks to watch her. Gram leaned into
Lexi thinking she was whispering and said, "The
last time Brody and I played poker at Kak's, she
cheated. Honey, your grandfather and I were so
upset we went home and split a beer." Lexi rested
her hand on Doris' arm.

"I miss him, too, Gram."

Kak squeezed in next to Doris who had to move
to accommodate her enormous hat. Reaching
into her bag, Kak took out a flask and handed it
to Doris who smiled and shook her head.

The room became hushed as Father
MacIntosh, not pleased at the shortened mass
or by the people dressed as clowns or wearing
costumes from "The Fish Pirate's Daughter"
looking up at him from the pews, started his
remarks, talking fast:

"St. Therese of Lisieux reminds us of the importance of our family and how our home is a smaller version of the world. With love, empathy and respect for our families, we can be the change we want to see around us. If you want to bring happiness to the whole world, go home and love your family."

Lexi felt a pang of guilt for abandoning her grandparents to pursue a new life. Just then, the sun burst through the stained glass windows sending shafts of colored light into the church. Was this a sign? If it was, what was it a sign of? She could feel self-doubt creep in. Should she move home? Stop thinking about why and how her parents died? Forget about her friends, her found family?

Lexi had never known Brody to work and only had a vague sense of what he did so was surprised when the priest talked about how Brody came to Alaska as part of the Conservation Corps during the transfer of totem poles to public parks designated for their display.

He wasn't the best guy for the job, she thought, because, as far as Lexi knew, and very much unlike Doris, he did not show any interest in Native culture. According to Father MacIntosh, Brody got the job done and gave himself credit when it became a tourist destination. Father McIntosh nodded to Doris, who must have insisted he tell the story of the totem poles, as he told the crowd that once the Native populations were pushed off the coasts and into cities to find work since their way of life was cut off, the totem poles, markers of the clans, of stories and, the tallest poles reserved for memorials and clan identifiers, rotted in the forests until the state decided to collect and preserve them.

Doris was pleased. She even clapped.

Throughout the service, Doris turned to Lexi periodically and asked loudly "What is he saying?" There was no need for a response. Lexi just smiled at her grandmother and looked sheepishly at Father MacIntosh. Despite his best efforts, the service went over Doris' schedule by half an hour.

Once the service was over, some people milled about in the aisles, but most left to set up the parade. Lexi needed to throw on her clown suit but was hoping her grandmother would let her off the hook.

Doris went to the bathroom as Lexi hung around the vestibule pretending to look at the flyers posted on a cork board. She could feel someone behind her and turned to find Ross standing in front of her, smiling.

"Thank you for coming," Lexi said.

"Of course," Ross said.

Lexi could feel the color on her cheeks thinking of Ross watching her parade down Front Street in a clown suit. She asked, "You aren't going to the parade are you?"

"No. That's not our thing." Lexi nodded.

"Oh good," she stammered. "I mean, I understand. I'll be the one in a clown suit with a hula hoop for a body."

"That is the one thing I wish I were seeing today." Ross laughed. "You might see Dot. She's always loved the parade and her parents have never been as militant as mine."

Doris came toward them and Ross waved before melting into a group of people leaving the church.

Doris asked, "Who was that Native kid?"

"He's not a kid." Lexi answered. "It's Ross. I went to school with him. And he's Tlingit."

Doris smiled, proud that Lexi had been listening those times she sat waiting for the end of the museum tour

As they were headed outside, Lexi saw her grandmother's energy flag and decided to ask her about the bat phone in the Mayor's office to take her mind off the finality of the funeral.

"How do you know about that? Oh–" she interrupted herself. "Carl. He's too clever for his own good."

Lexi walked Doris to a bench under the notice board. "Tell me about it."

"You know I worked for Alaska Telecom Systems run by the Air Force back in the day. Alaska had so much empty space between towns that no private company would run lines so the military ran the lines along existing telegraph lines. That was true for the entire country at the turn of the century." Doris stood. "We have to get going."

Lexi opened the front door and they stepped outside. People nodded to her as they passed. She nodded back as she continued to talk. "So the Army strung the telegraph lines in the east and the Air Force ran the lines in the west. And Billy Mitchell was our man in the west. My boss."

She explained how the line in the Mayor's office must have been set up in case of emergency without thinking to have a record of the calls so no mechanism for billing was ever attached to it. It was as if the calls did not exist.

"Keep it under your hat," she said conspiratorially. "I'm sure that phone was supposed to be discontinued ages ago."

As they walked toward the start of the parade, Doris suggested they walk back to the house where Lexi could change. Lexi did not believe there was time but it was her grandmother's day.

As they walked slowly up the stairs to the house, a stray dog followed. There were always a lot of loose dogs on the streets and, like the other kids in town, Lexi learned about the birds and the bees watching them mate. It made her chuckle to think of it.

Once at the house, Lexi opened the front door. Doris entered first, walked out of her shoes, leaving them abandoned in the doorway. Lexi ran upstairs to change. The clown outfit was wrinkled from her bag. She shook it out and put it on. She looked ridiculous but, she thought, that was the point. In the bathroom, she put white paint on her face, put big red dots on her cheeks and blue teardrops below her eyes. Another sad clown. She didn't remember ever being a happy clown. The few pictures of her as a little kid confirmed it: she had large, red frown lines around her mouth and big blue tears painted below her eyes. Leaving her purse behind, she threw on her tennis shoes and walked downstairs.

Doris sat at the kitchen table drinking a cold cup of coffee left over from the morning. Lexi sat down. The parade was starting but she did not want to rush her grandmother. Lexi's mind wandered, thinking about what she learned about her parents since coming home. More than she had ever known before. She realized she was staring at the plastic cups lining the windowsill. Each cup had an avocado pit in varying stages of growth. Some with leaves, others had thin roots dipping into the stale water, but more were dead.

"Did you see how Kak went up to Father McIntosh?" asked Doris, bringing Lexi back from her reverie. "She doesn't even believe. Trying to suck up the air at Brody's funeral. If I get like that, shoot me."

"Don't you think you're being hard on Kak?" Lexi was surprised at how negative Doris was acting lately toward her oldest friend. "She's been going to your church for as long as I've been alive so why wouldn't she talk to the priest?"

"You might have a point." Doris finished her coffee. "I just can't believe we just buried your grandfather."

Lexi leaned over and put her hand on her shoulder. The parade was just a distraction. "I know, Gram."

"When I was working, Kak used to watch you and take you down to the pier to collect coins at low tide.

"I remember it being fun. You'd be surprised how much money the drunks would drop. Sometimes whole dollars that we'd dry on the stove."

Doris stood up. "We'd better get a move on or we'll miss the parade. You look great, kid."

Even though it didn't sit well with Lexi to dress as a clown and blow a kazoo just after Brody's funeral, Doris was smiling and waving at her friends, on the sidewalk and in the parade. She was enjoying having her way now that Brody was gone. Lexi was proud of her. Brody had ruled the roost. It always felt as if they were humoring him, but that did not mean he was not getting his way. Now Gram was stretching her wings and Lexi smiled thinking about how it was Doris's turn to push her around.

It was an unusually bright day. Clouds of mosquitoes hung in the air as the sun's heat warmed the wooden boards along the parade route on Front Street. The air rising off the wood turned to mist.

Deciding to lean into the whole clown thing, Lexi brushed her curly hair into a large red ball of fuzz and tied pieces of striped ribbon on strands of hair.

Doris said, "stop clowning around and come over." She gave Lexi a peck on the cheek before joining Kak on the sidewalk.

The parade was originally put together by the theater group, the First City Players. There wasn't that much to do in town so the Drum & Kazoo parade became a tradition. Everyone came in costume. At the start of the parade a man sat at a piano on a wheeled platform. As soon as he started to play, the piano moved and he grabbed his bench and ran to catch up. A scene Lexi remembered well.

A few of the actors from the "The Fish Pirate's Daughter" melodrama came in costumes, the villain twirled his cape as he curled his mustache, Little Nell, the ringleted heroine, running for her life. Snidely Whiplash would catch Little Nell and tie her to imaginary railway tracks before getting rescued by Dudley Do-Right at intervals every half a block.

Lexi's group, the clowns, played kazoos and toy drums. The Veterans brought up the rear, cheered by the crowd.

The parade was over almost as soon as it had begun because Downtown Ketchikan was only a few blocks long. Lexi was hot and sweating in her clown suit. Her makeup was melting and the smell of the mosquito repellant was making her feel slightly nauseous. As they rounded the corner on Main street, she saw Carl with his boyfriend Felix and perked up. They were not holding hands but it was obvious to someone in the know that they were together.

Carl called, "Your curls!"

Felix gave a weak wave. Lexi raised her shoulders and pointed to Felix. "What's up with him?"

Carl said, "He's not happy with himself today."

Lexi yelled "Is that code for 'hungover?'"

Carl laughed. "Clever you. San Francisco has sharpened your claws."

Lexi waved and blew a kiss. The end of the parade was in sight. Lexi caught motion down a side street, it was Margaret having what looked like an argument with Bob Kincaid. She wasn't far from where they were standing but the noise of the drums and the kazoos surrounding her drowned out all other sound.

She stopped in the middle of the street to watch. Another clown walked into her, nearly knocking her over. The kids on the sidewalks laughed thinking it was a routine. Lexi joined the rest of the parade participants at the end of the block.

Clouds had formed and it started to rain in earnest. Firecrackers fizzled in the damp air. Everyone got soaked.

19

In what continues to be the longest day, Lexi finds herself, after a funeral and a parade, at her grandfather's wake at her godmother's home overlooking the harbor. This night, on the 4th of July, would end with a big bang.

L exi was late to the wake. She had run home to change and wash her face. She put on the same black dress she wore to the funeral. Her hair was a non-starter so she put a scarf over her teased hair that ballooned under the scarf. Even though it was twilight in the summer light this far north, she put on sunglasses and left the house.

Kak's house was built on the side of Deer Mountain with large picture windows that looked out over the narrows. It had been raining since the end of the parade. As Lexi walked into Kak's house looking like a wet Jackie O, the crowd stopped talking and stared at her.

It seemed as if everyone in Ketchikan was crammed into Kak's small home. Lexi saw her old teachers, the parents of her classmates, Mrs. Dunnigan the principal, nuns and priests, neighbors, firefighters, politicians, and those were the people she recognized. There were plenty that she did not know from Adam.

She tried to skirt the wall and disappear but Kak spied her and motioned for her to join her on the sofa.

Taking off her sunglasses, Lexi said a quick hello, took her thumb and pinkie forming a pretend bottle and held it to her mouth, then pointed to the kitchen and made her way there. She saw her high school English teacher, Mr. LeBlanc, in a cue for the makeshift bar on the kitchen counter.

He frowned. "It sucks about your grandfather."

Lexi was taken aback. She had never heard Mr. LeBlanc speak like a regular person. She giggled, embarrassed, as heat came to her face.

"There's no easy way to say it," Mr. LeBlanc seemed to understand. "I believe that if it comes from your heart, it's the right thing to say. Death or grief. It comes to us all." It was odd to talk to him outside the classroom.

Lexi gave him the side eye. "I see you're as dramatic as ever." In school, in order to get the class to settle down, Mr. LeBlanc would climb on his desk and quote Shakespeare.

He felt an opening and walked through it. "The grief that does not speak knits up the o'er wrought heart and bids it break." He bowed deeply. "The Scottish play."

"Thank you." Lexi wanted to hug him. Though his antics made the class groan, Mr. LeBlanc was everyone's favorite teacher.

"I hear you made it to San Francisco." It was sweet that he remembered. In high school Lexi worked her job at the old folks home after school to save up. She was determined to graduate and leave Ketchikan behind. Mr. LeBlanc pulled out the map and asked each of the students to show where they would travel to after graduation. Lexi had pointed to San Francisco.

She finally made it to the head of the line and asked Bob, who was acting as bartender, for a drink. Spotting orange juice she asked for a screwdriver. She thanked Mr. LeBlanc for the talk and made her way out of the kitchen; she could hear Kak holding court.

When Lexi was young, she thought Kak was unbearable. Everything about her screamed for attention. She had always seemed old. She swept her thick bottle-red hair into a messy bun. Her makeup was heavy, her false eyelashes a monument to her youth.

After spending time in San Francisco where drag queens celebrated women like Kak, Lexi had a fresh appreciation for her flamboyance and rough charm.

Lexi bobbed between people, finally reaching the sofa.

"Well I'll be damned," Kak said. "The prodigal daughter returns." Now that she had an audience, Kak made a sweeping gesture toward Lexi.

"I just saw you at breakfast." Lexi said with good humor as she sunk into the couch next to Kak. "And 'prodigal' means I wasted money, but, I grant you, it sounds impressive."

Lexi took off her sunglasses and put them in her clutch.

Doris was sitting in an armchair next to the couch nursing a Dubonnet. She smiled at her granddaughter cheerfully but Lexi noticed that her eyes were unfocused from the drink.

Trailing cigarette ashes as she spoke, and for the hundredth time, Kak told the story about how her husband bought his first new car, a Chrysler, in 1953.

"He drove that car into the garage, turned off the key and died of a heart attack sitting in the driver's seat." Kak said merrily, nearly spilling her drink. Once the polite laughter died down, she turned to Lexi and asked, "What happened to that cat of yours? What's his name?"

Lexi, squeezed between Kak and a stranger on the couch said, "She. And her name is Saxman Bight, as you know."

Kak let out a cackle that could knock a person over. "You are so weird."

Lexi was happy to be teased by Kak who knew about Saxman but never let facts get in the way of a good ribbing. It cheered Doris up. Kak would be an anchor for her now. An anchor that would become unmoored at times, but an anchor nonetheless.

"Saxman's still with us?" Kak asked.

Doris looked up from the group; ignoring Kak, she addressed Lexi, "There you are. You and your grandfather would go 18 rounds over toilet paper."

Kak interrupted. "That cat of yours—" This was how things went with Kak and Doris. "Saxman!"

Kak roared. "What kind of name is that? Who names a cat after a national park?" She threw her head back with a husky laugh. "That cat loved toilet paper. There were always bits of the stuff all over the house."

Lexi finished the story. "I would put the toilet paper on the back of the toilet so she couldn't get to it and Brody would say, 'That's not how we live in this house and put it back on the roll.'" Everyone laughed.

Mr. LeBlanc said, from behind the couch, "How are your cats, Catherine?"

Kak turned her head to blow smoke away from the group but there were people everywhere. "My two little darlings."

"Just the two these days?"

"Just the two. They all die in the end. I have Cunningham and Wakefield left. I named them after my dead husband's law firm. I like to yell their names when they're bad. Vincent would have loathed that."

Doris asked Lexi, "Who's watching Saxman now?"

"One of my bakery friends, Henry." She imagined it must be a mess at his apartment since his eyes weren't their best and, at 20 years old, neither were Saxman's. She hoped others in her little group would come and help Henry out.

"Who is Henry?" Doris' question opened a can of worms Lexi wanted closed. She didn't want to discuss it, but she had had a few drinks, and she was weary of explaining, again, who her San Francisco friends where.

"A friend."

"If that creature is still alive, what does that make me?" Kak said in her best smoker's voice. A rasp from hell. "God, that makes her, what? Twenty years old?" She took a deep drag. "Do cats live that long?" Smoke curled out of her mouth as she spoke.

Lexi laughed. Kak would fit in well with her eccentric friends in San Francisco. "They do in San Francisco. She's an indoor cat."

"Why?" Kak pretended she had never heard of an indoor animal.

"Because she's very old." Lexi answered. "She doesn't make it out of the kitchen most days."

Kak put her arm around Lexi's shoulder and pulled her even closer. "It's a good thing you came home. It's been too long."

Lexi noticed Doris leaning forward.

"Gram, what are you doing?" Lexi's grandmother was peering at her leg through her reading glasses. She had tweezers in her hand and paused to look at Lexi. "Your grandfather loved a smooth leg."

"Why don't you just shave?"

"You've got to be gentle with the old skin. You can rip your legs to shreds with a razor." She went back to plucking the few hairs Lexi could not even see on her leg. "I want him to have one last look at smooth legs cause I'm never doing it again."

Once freed of Kak and Doris, Lexi leaned against the open sliding glass door to the back porch overlooking the harbor, the narrows stretching as far as she could see. The sky was clearing, the air chilly. There were a lot of conversations in the noisy room behind her, but one voice was clear. She heard someone say, "June married that guy, Terry. Flying that plane half in the bag." Lexi's drink slipped from her hand and crashed to the floor. She looked around to see who had been talking but a crowd had formed around her.

Margaret sprung into action. "Let me get that." She piled the large pieces of glass into her palm and asked Johnny to bring a dustpan and a broom.

Felix came to Lexi's rescue. He pulled her away as she thanked Margaret and Johnny for cleaning up her mess.

Like most people at the wake, Felix was three sheets to the wind. He corralled her into a corner and proceeded to tell her how much he loved Carl.

"It's— you know—the same way only music can make you feel sometimes. Like you're full. You know, brimming with feeling. That's what Carl gives me. I don't want to leave here. It's where we fell in love. It's our home." He was pleading.

"Please stop encouraging us to come to San Francisco. I don't want to lose him."

Lexi tried to reassure him. "But Carl loves you."

"It's not that. There's too much temptation. He could get sick."

Lexi understood.

Felix said, "I'll drop it." He was tearing up. Lexi hugged him.

She left Felix to look for Carl who was leaning on the kitchen counter talking to Bob.

"Carl." Lexi called, joining him.

"God, your grandparents–" Carl swung around to face her. "It's hard to think of Doris without Brody."

"Or you without Felix."

Carl looked perplexed. "Okay." Bob started talking to someone else so Carl went behind the counter and made Lexi another screwdriver. She took a sip. "I have so much to tell you."

"Get to it before another mourner hones in on us to tell you how sad it is that–" He paused and Lexi filled in the blank.

"an 89-year-old—"

"—passed away unexpectedly." They giggled, falling into each other like kids. Once they had recovered, Lexi gave Carl the once over. "Now you're dressing like a lumberjack. Throwing it in Felix's face."

"I'll explain later." Carl said, teasing: "And you look like a bedraggled Jackie O or a demented Holly Golightly." He made a Brandy Alexander for himself. They said together: "Never mix, never worry" and clinking glasses.

Lexi said, "I know you always thought Mr. LeBlanc was straight when we were in high school but how about now?"

Carl laughed. "I wish. He's such a sweetheart. Not every interesting man is gay; though most are."

"It's confusing up here." Lexi said. "You can really tell who's gay in San Francisco. The closet is pretty wide open."

"Now." Carl took a sip of his drink. "Tell me everything. How much money did Doris and Kak find stashed around the house?"

"Enough to stop them from thinking I took it all for our trips to the five and dime when we were kids." She took a sip of her drink. "It was thousands. They paid for my ticket up here. But that's not the headline." Lexi took a slow, dramatic drink. "I found my mother's diary."

"No!"

"That's just the subheadline."

Carl gasped.

"There's part of it in code and you have to help decipher it."

Carl was delighted. "I haven't worn my code breaker hat for a while. Remember how we sent each other coded messages but none of us could remember the codes and could never decipher them."

Carl took Lexi by the elbow and guided her to a quiet corner. "Where is said diary?"

Lexi explained that Doris didn't let her bring her book bag to the wake, but she would bring it to his apartment the next night. She told him about Ruby Sylvester and Professor Parker. She was going to Ruby's house the next day.

"I'm so nervous."

"I would be, too," Carl said. "She could be a murderer. You said she knows how to fly now?"

"She became a pilot after her brother and dad died. She went to Anchorage to get her license."

"Oh." Carl hesitated. "She obviously didn't want to take flying lessons from Terry."

"Who is this professor?"

"Samantha Parker." Feeling tipsy, Lexi leaned against the wall. "I'm not sure there's anything to it. She worked for the oil companies. Apparently doing environmental impact studies nowhere near the pipeline. It was just something weird Bob said. And what about Rey? Maybe she didn't just let June go after she married my father?"

Kak called from the other room, "Lexi! I need you, darling."

Carl leaned close to Lexi and said, "Give Kak a parrot on her shoulder to get the attention she craves. Maybe your clown suit is available."

"She's harmless. Though I will say that even in San Francisco, Kak would be over-the-top. Come on, you've always loved Kak."

"True." Carl acquiesced. "I don't mind a little blood in the water. You can't get more camp than Kak." Lexi gave Carl a peck on the cheek. "Hey, I thought you never went to the parade?" He broke into a smile. "We hate that parade, but we honestly wanted to see if you would be forced to go." He laughed. "And in a clown outfit no less. Priceless."

He turned serious. "The question is, why were you there?"

Lexi said, "According to Doris, I am not a grown woman."

"Clearly you are not a grown anything, because you can't say no to your grandmother." As Carl and Lexi talked they walked into the living room as a rainbow appeared outside the open sliding glass doors.

"On cue!" Carl said, gesturing to the sky.

A few hours later, Kak was not in her spot on the couch, now leaning on a chair near the back porch. She motioned for Lexi to come to her.

Just then they heard the popping of the first fireworks in the harbor, set off from the deck of a few boats in the middle of the narrows. Since the 4th of July was one of the longest days in the summer this far north, the fireworks started around 10 o'clock at night when just a little light was left from the sinking sun. It had long stopped raining and the sky cleared. The sky filled with blooming fireworks, the crackle of the explosions distorted in the air.

20

Lexi remembers drunken conversations and nervously prepares to meet Ruby Sylvester.

Lexi woke with a killer hangover. In her foggy mind, the days since she arrived home were starting to run together, contributed to by the fact that it stays light until midnight in the summer. Without a work schedule or an actual vacation with daytime plans, it felt like an endless summer. The funeral was over, the 4th behind her, the wake or party or whatever it was at Kak's all turned into one endless day.

It was late. The display next to her bed read 1:00 p.m. She strained to hear Doris but it was deadly quiet. She threw on tights, Doc Martens, and a pull-over sweater. Downstairs was quiet. She grabbed a slicker and went for a walk to clear her head.

A few snippets of conversations after too many vodkas came back to her. She was sitting on the couch squeezed next to Kak and a few of the First City Players, who had not changed their outfits from the parade.

Lexi asked Kak about Terry leaving the Sylvester family on Admiralty Island, but immediately regretted it because Kak protested loudly that Terry was pursued by "that daughter" for years. That there was nothing to it, and that Ruth had no basis for her claims.

She managed to free herself from Kak's orbit by offering to bring her a fresh martini. As she reached the kitchen, Lexi could hear Margaret talking. She stopped just outside the door to listen. Margaret was telling someone about how she had checked the plane the morning of the crash and "there was nothing wrong with it." Margaret had admitted as much to her at the bar.

What she said next was a revelation. "But someone tinkered with it." Margaret whispered. "I have theories of how it could have been done deliberately." When Lexi walked into the kitchen the conversation stopped.

Lexi asked, "Why would someone want to hurt my parents?"

Margaret rushed to Lexi and gave her a hug. "I'm so sorry about Brody."

"Thank you." Lexi said, confused by Margaret's effusiveness since she had seen her at the bar the other day.

"What were you saying about the plane?"

"Oh nothing." She said with a dismissive wave of her hand.

Lexi looked from Magaret nursing a drink to Bob who was serving them. "What were you and Bob fighting about at the parade?"

"We weren't fighting" Margaret said with a lighthearted flick of her hair. "Bob pointed out, and not for the first time, that I have to stop piecing the plane together at the hangar. It's my Frankenstein's monster." She looked at Bob who agreed. "He's right. I need to move on. It was an accident. I hate to say it but planes go down up here all the time. The weather is terrible. There were freak storms for October, like a winter Takus."

"Takus?"

"It's a strong nor'easter. Very cold. Brutal."

"But they don't come that time of the year," Kak said, walking in behind the group in the kitchen. "A Takus is more of a February storm." She turned to Lexi. "Forget my drink?"

Lexi was unsteady and pretty drunk by that point in the evening but she remembered thinking: Was there a storm when her parents plane went down or not? Margaret obviously didn't want to upset her by talking about it at her grandfather's wake.

Everyone knew that Margaret was married to her high school sweetheart Johnny, who had many rough years with drink and drugs. In another conversation, Lexi remembered standing next to Carl and overhearing someone say, "Why does she stay with him? He's always on the sauce." Carl responded, "Word is he's a great lover." Lexi blushed and protested. "Maybe, but she does love him."

She needed to think and walked to the docks and back, the entire length of the downtown, ending up in front of the police station on Front Street. It was close to 5:00 p.m.

Colette was sitting at the front desk typing on a Selectric.

Lexi leaned over the front counter and said, "You look official in your uniform."

Colette looked up and smiled. "I am official. Officer Nelson to you."

"Officer Colette Nelson of the Ketchikan Police Department." They hugged and Colette motioned for her to sit next to the desk.

"Is this a friendly visit or an official one?"

"A little of both. I'm looking for information on the Jim's Lake incident in 1956 and on my parents' plane crash in 1965."

"What do you want to know about Jim's Lake for?"

"I know the daughter always blamed my father for not picking her family up. I know there's nothing to it but people have been saying my parents' plane crash wasn't an accident and I'm just wondering."

"Alexandra," Colette said sternly. "You shouldn't be digging into anything like this."

"I'm not digging." She crossed her fingers behind her purse. "I just want to read something official about what happened. We only heard rumors about what happened to the Sylvester family. I don't think I ever put it together that my father was supposed to pick them up." Lexi could see Colette was skeptical.

"You know nobody talked about my parents when I was a kid."

"Other than to tease you about it." Colette said sympathetically.

"Mercilessly, but that's okay. You, Ross and Carl all stuck up for me."

"My family stayed up at Jim's Lake once during summer break. We just took our boat and stayed on the banks of the island living off the land." Colette smiled at the memory. "That is ancient forest up there. There's great hunting in the Kootznoowoo forest and the fish practically jump into your boat on the lake, where the Sylvesters were, but we didn't get that far. It's very remote and the island is lousy with bears."

"I'll see what I can do about the report," Collette continued. "There was no investigation by the police since it was search and rescue by the Coast Guard, but I have a cousin in the Coast Guard."

"Of course you do," Lexi said. They laughed.

"Sit tight." Colette stood up. "Let me look for anything I might have for those dates. It's slim pickings in the files." She asked for the dates again and disappeared into a back office.

Lexi fidgeted in her seat. She picked up a photo of the Nelson clan on Colette's desk. There were at last 20 people in the picture dressed in Haida regalia. A grass hat, or black felt with fringe, black and red felt capes with mother of pearl buttons sewn into the shape of what Lexi knew was an elaborate raven on the back of the capes, the Nelson clan animal. A few of the elders wore woven blankets with images of black bears and long thick fringe.

She set the picture back as Colette returned to the front office.

"I found," Colette said as Lexi looked up expectantly, "nothing I'm afraid."

Lexi did not hide her disappointment.

"But I promise I'll call my cousin and whatever she finds I'll get a copy to you."

"I don't want Doris to know I'm even a little bit interested so can you give the information to Carl?"

Colette agreed.

"Thank you Officer Nelson." Lexi said, giving her a squeeze before leaving for home.

The weather turned from warm to cold. It was evening, but still light, when she walked through the front door. The smell of bacon grease hung in the air, the television blared, the curtains were drawn but the windows were open. The cold was like a slap to the face.

She stepped over Doris's discarded shoes, rain boots, and jackets that had fallen off hooks in the hall and walked into the living room. Gram was in her recliner asleep, the glow from the television the only light in the dark room. She looked at the sofa where her grandfather always sat. A faded blue towel where his head used to rest was still there. Of all the things to keep after Doris and Kak had a clean out, that ratty towel struck Lexi as the saddest.

Lexi turned off the television, which woke Doris. Startled, she sat up nearly propelling her small frame onto the floor.

"Lexi!"

"Hi Gram," Lexi gave her grandmother a hug. She seemed smaller than even yesterday. She had never thought of her grandmother as frail but here she was hugging the bird bones of the woman that raised her.

Gram said, "I was resting my eyes." Lexi smiled.

Gram asked Lexi to make her a pot of coffee. "Not that motor oil you drink. Folgers is fine for me."

In the kitchen, Lexi noticed layers of dirt and grease on the countertops for the first time since she came home. The stove had not been scrubbed in some time. No matter how much her grandmother said she was fine, this showed the opposite.

21

Lexi visits with Ruby Sylvester and takes a terrifying plane ride with a potential killer.

The Sylvester home was a large square box. It was dark inside, the curtains were drawn. Once her eyes adjusted Lexi saw that it was spotless and sparse. A few pieces of furniture, an old rug. It looked as if nothing had been touched since her family died.

Lexi found herself staring at Ruby, pretty and outdoorsy, long blonde hair glowing in the low light.

Ruby motioned for Lexi to sit. "Tea?" Lexi shook her head.

"Thank you for seeing me."

"I only agreed because I want to set you straight. Your father murdered my family."

Lexi pulled the article from her pocket before sitting. "But this quotes the Coast Guard. They investigated. There was a storm that kept my father's plane grounded."

"And who wrote that article?" Ruby said triumphantly. Lexi glanced at the byline.

"Bob Kinkaid."

"Exactly." Ruby was leaning toward Lexi. There was so much space between the chairs that the effect was more odd than it was menacing. "I am a pilot and I fly in weather exactly like the conditions on that day."

"How could it be exact?" Lexi could see Ruby was not having a discussion but a monologue.

"Your father killed my family."

"For what it's worth," Lexi stood. "I am so sorry that you lost them, but your father and brother were on a raft when the storm came up. Even if my father had been able to land, he might not have been able to rescue them."

"You can't understand." Ruby contained her rage with a menacing whisper. She stood up abruptly. "I'll take you out to see where they died. You owe me that."

Lexi didn't feel she owed Ruby anything, but she did know what it was like to lose family so she agreed.

As she followed Ruby out of the empty house, Lexi wondered how far Ruby's anger would take her.

They drove to the hangar outside town in Ruby's old Chrysler that had to be 30 years old. Likely the Sylvester family car.

It was chilly and a light rain started. There were two buildings side by side. Lexi shivered when she realized the closed hangar next to them must be where the wreckage from her parents plane was housed.

Ruby strode to the open hangar where a two-seater Cessna sat in the middle of the large space. She opened the plane door and motioned for Lexi to climb in first and take the back seat behind the pilot.

Lexi's stomach tightened as she scrambled to step into the plane and struggled to get into the seat. She put on the helmet that was on the seat and strapped in.

Ruby took her seat in the front and started the engine. The propellers spun and the engine roared as Ruby taxied to the airstrip. The rain was coming down hard as they bounced their way off the ground.

Lexi took deep breaths. She thought Ruby was talking to her but could hear nothing but the engine and the rain pummeling the plane. Lexi wondered what she was trying to prove by agreeing to come. That she was not afraid? Because she was very afraid.

The plane banked sharply as it circled and headed north. It was bumpy and Lexi's pulse quickened as the plane climbed.

Lexi looked at her watch, and was shocked to realize they had been flying for over an hour when the plane suddenly took a dive, coming close to the trees below. Ruby pointed to a lake Lexi assumed was the one Ruby's father and brother were on when the storm came up, Jim's Lake.

As quickly as the plane descended, it rose into the air. Lexi felt sick from the motion. She was relieved when the plane turned around and headed back south.

By the time the plane landed, the rain was pouring. Lexi was wobbly as she exited the plane behind Ruby, who jumped to the ground, energized. Ruby took her helmet off and shook her hair out. She had a look of triumph on her face.

She waited for Ruby to say something as they stood in the hangar.

"That was the lake. If we were in a seaplane, a Beaver," she said with emphasis, "We could have landed on the lake."

"Except that this is not a storm." Lexi said gently. "This is rain."

"You don't know," Ruby's voice was a roar. Lexi blanched. "I was on that island and I heard their cries."

"I am so sorry."

"Don't!" Ruby cut her off.

Knowing she might never see Ruby again, Lexi waited until she calmed down before asking. "Were you in town on October 19, 1965?"

Ruby smiled. "You don't think it was an accident." Her laugh was ugly. "I wish I'd thought of it. I was getting my masters at the University of Fairbanks."

Lexi did not relax until she was home. The first thing she did was call information for the number for the university. It was summer but she hoped someone would be working during summer school that could answer her question.

22

A romantic picnic with Ross takes Lexi's mind off what is now a full blown investigation into her parents' untimely death. They lay out a blanket at the accurately named Buggy Beach on the shores of Ward Lake.

Ross had asked Lexi to take a drive to Ward Lake. He picked her up at the bottom of the stairs.

"You still have the old Indian?" Lexi ran to the motorcycle. It's military-green body low to the ground. The leather seat, cracked and worn.

"Yeah," Ross followed her to the bike. "My grandfather finally gave it to me—once I showed him I could keep it going." He stroked the bike affectionately. "There aren't any parts for it. I have to beg Maggie to jerry rig it when it breaks down. It's basically spit and wire."

"Remember how me and Carl used to tease you about riding an 'Indian.' What little shits we were."

Ross looked at Lexi and smiled. His hair fell over his eyes as he swept it back with his hand. He said, "It was funny, at the time." Ross sat on the bike. "Hop on."

It was warm. Lexi sat on the back of the bike and put her arms around Ross. Revving the engine, they took off to Higgins Road away from the water. It started to sprinkle. Lexi turned her face to the sky and let the water drop onto her face and hair.

They turned north toward Ward Lake, quickly leaving the center of town, driving along Tongass Highway. Ketchikan hugged the shore for six miles; ascending the mountain for about four miles from the shoreline along the base of Deer Mountain.

They rode past Totem Bight State Park where Lexi saw Ross dance when she first arrived in town.

Ross slowed before turning onto Revilla Road. The drive reminded Lexi of the ride she had had with Jerry through Marin to the beach where they enjoyed a lunch Jerry packed, then continued on to Manka Inn where they spent the night. She put Jerry out of her mind and hugged Ross closer. Lexi could smell the earthy rain on the pavement, spruce and hemlock trees, and a whiff of skunk cabbage made her feel at home.

As they wound their way along the highway, they saw the only cemetery in Ketchikan. A woman was washing a gravestone with a bucket and soapy water. Lexi wondered why someone would wash a gravestone in the rain? She glimpsed a row of snapdragons that outlined a small patch just below the headstone before the scene disappeared behind a crop of trees. A child, she thought.

The rain stopped just as they reached the lake. Lexi recognized the rocky beach and the trees that came right to the edge of the water on the far side but she didn't remember the beauty. As a kid, she was not happy when a class picnic was scheduled at the leach-filled lake. Her memories were tainted by a bee that came out of nowhere to sting her on the forehead and the school bully pushing her into the dirt.

They were not all bad memories. There was tubing down Fish Creek in summer and sledding in winter.

Lexi and Ross dismounted the Indian and walked up the path to the small beach. They took off their jackets, laying them down on the rocks before sitting down. The water reflected the trees and the surrounding mountains as the sun came through the clouds; steam rose from the rocks, the scent of fresh rain surrounded them.

"It's so beautiful."

Lexi gazed at the water. "You just don't see it when you live here. You might have." She looked at Ross and asked. "Did you always know?"

"Not me, either." Ross waved his hand in front of him. "I only saw it after coming back from college. I sat right here. And I saw it."

"Funny that." Lexi said as they looked from the lake to each other. "Come see our band." Lexi gave him a quizzical look. "Me, Dot, Carl. Remember we messed around in high school. Now we have a Journey cover band."

"No way." Lexi wanted to punch his arm the way her friend Stella did for emphasis. "Of course I'd love to come."

"You should join us. Do you still play?"

Lexi thought back to plucking "Don't Bring Me Down" on her acoustic guitar with her friends in Ross's garage. "ELO all the way, man."

"Dot on drums. You on base. Me and Car on guitar."

"We were terrible." Lexi giggled.

"We picked the easiest songs." They both played air guitar and sang "Don't bring me down. No. No. No. No. No."

They settled into listening to the birds and the buzz of insects enjoying sitting near each other.

Lexi broke the silence and asked about the woman washing the gravestones.

A little gravel entered Ross's otherwise pleasant voice. "Alice washes the tombstones of her children every day rain or shine. They were taken from her by the Canadian government and put into schools."

"Like your Uncle Johnny."

Ross nodded gravely. "She is between worlds. She converted to Catholicism but lost her children because of it. You know what happened to them." It was Lexi's time to nod. "Many of them disappeared."

"The children aren't in the graves if they were taken."

Ross nodded. "No. Her children never returned. It broke her and now she's touched and washes the graves of other children who died many years before her children were born."

Ross stood up and extended his hand to Lexi. She jumped up, landing in his arms. After a long, warm hug he said, "Let's walk."

It was a good day for eagle sightings. Several large eagles sat on the tops of Sitka trees while others circled slowly overhead. They watched for some time before Ross said, "Ketchikan is actually a Tlingit word, Kach Khanna. It means 'spread wings of the eagle.' The tourists learn that the city was named after Ketchikan creek but it's Kach Khanna."

"I have heard that many times from Doris. She won't let the tourists leave the tour until they can pronounce 'Kach Khanna.'" Lexi was pleased Ross was laughing.

"I wish we had learned any of that in school."

Ross said, "We only knew what they taught us. I was in college before I learned what little I could about the Haida language and my people, but that's all changing. Every year we take more of our culture back."

Lexi sat up. "The headdress," she whispered. Ross only smiled. She knew then that Ross understood who had taken the headdress and probably returned it to the tribe it belonged to that lived in the plains of the midwest.

Lexi thought about what it meant to have to fight to keep your culture. "Doris still strong arms tourists with her lecture on Indians. Their eyes glaze over."

Ross said, "Your grandmother suffers from 'noble savage' syndrome." His voice was gentle, his eyes laughing. "When they're not trying to kill us and take away anything sacred, they're making Indians out to be as brave and superhuman as Superman. If we were just people to your grandmother, some of us would be respected and some would be ignored, just like everybody else. We don't need your adulation."

"Guilty." Lexi met Ross's gaze. "How many times did we take a bus to the lodge and see the button dance show and it never got through to me that it wasn't a show." She paused, "Isn't a show."

Ross completed her thought. "It's an ancient ritual about nature that supports the community. We enact it with the same goal as our ancestors."

They walked past fire pits built long ago, logs arranged as seats to drink beer taken from unsuspecting parents. Lexi pointed to Ross who laughed since they had done the same thing when they were in school. They sat on one of the logs.

Lexi said, "I remember when we were kids, Doris and Kak took me and Dot for a swim. They brought lunch: a box of raisins and peanut butter and jelly sandwiches. I put tiny crabs into the empty raisin box. When we got home, I forgot about the crabs and Doris put the raisin box away and was closing the cabinet when she heard scraping from inside the box. When she opened it, tiny crabs crawled out." Ross ducked in mock horror.

"Doris made us ride our bikes to the ocean and release those baby crabs back into the water."

They grinned at each other as Ross stood, extending his hand. Lexi took his hand and blushed. This was the kid she climbed trees with, ran around Totem Bight with, staring at the carved faces of Bear, Raven and Frog, and, along with his cousin Dot, ate seaweed dried on his grandmother's porch. The man smiling at her today was lean and tall, brown as tree bark. His black hair in a braid sat heavy down his back. He left her breathless.

Ross leaned in and kissed her. They made out like teenagers for a long while before leaving the beach and entering the woods surrounding the lake. He pointed out the spruce and cottonwood, birch and poplar, Red Alders and hemlock. Lexi was not surprised he knew so much. His family and Margaret's had been carvers for centuries. They sat on a fallen log next to blueberry bushes and mushroom stools, the familiar scent of damp earth and moss surrounding them.

Ross stood. "My ass is getting wet." As they walked they stepped over more fallen trees covered in lichen that was in the process of being absorbed back into the woods.

"The algae and fungus work together in partnership." Ross said. "The fungus gathers moisture that the algae needs. You know, the fungus and trees are ancient friends."

"Kind of like you and me." Lexi said, stepping to avoid crushing a ring of mushrooms.

"Exactly." Ross gave Lexi's arm a squeeze. They couldn't stop touching each other. "Lichen can be used as a medicine. It's a natural antibiotic like pine sap. You can eat it, though I wouldn't risk it because it can also be poisonous. The one I remember from my great-grandmother was used as a dye. Back in the day, lichen yellows were really valuable." As they walked, Ross picked up sticks and put them in a hammock he made from a handkerchief.

"Where did you learn about lichen?"

"Mostly from my grandmother, but also in college. I studied ecology."

Ross talked of losing his grandmother and that was the reason he came home after college. The forest seemed to relax him. "She was the heart of the family and I wanted to keep everything she fought hard to preserve. Her brother was also taken. He was tender hearted and cried for his mother so they beat him. He hung himself."

"God, Ross." Lexi touched his arm. "I'm so sorry."

They sat in silence listening to the lapping of the water along the shore. An Eagle cried and seemed to wake them.

"I remember your grandmother so well. She scared the shit out of me."

Ross laughed, a deep belly laugh. "I'm not sure she'd be happy that I came back. Her goal was for us to go to law school and beat the white man at their own game."

He looked at Lexi. His eyes were shiny and sad.

"I think she would have been glad that you followed your heart home. Now you're the heart of the family."

He leaned toward her and kissed her tenderly. She relaxed into the embrace feeling very much at home.

Lexi thought that for others who have lost someone, there was a before and after the death, but for her there was only her life after. Ross had memories of his grandmother. Even Lexi remembered Grandmother Abrams' activism, her command, her love of her family. She was one of the only women Lexi ever saw drumming at the Potlatch ceremonies. Her voice was strong as she swayed to the rhythm, chanting. The button blanket she wore with the raven crest in abalone shells shining in the light as it moved gently around her.

They were walking when Ross stopped. "This is a good place to set up camp."

Lexi asked, "Did you bring me a fish?"

"No. I brought hot dogs." Ross opened his backpack and took out a package of Oscar Mayer hot dogs. He lit a fire as Lexi skewered the dogs onto sticks.

Ross reassured her. "The smoke should keep the mosquitoes away."

They roasted the hotdogs, grinning at each other like fools.

Once she bit into the smokey meat, Lexi thought it was the best hot dog she ever had.

Lexi grilled Ross on what had changed since she moved away. Was the curiosity shop with shells and bits of beach debris with a few faded birthday cards in the window still there? He nodded.

"I saw the polar bear outside the post office." She said. "She's looking sad." Ross growled like they used to do as kids when they walked past the bear.

They sat in silence for a moment listening to the birds and watching the still lake. Ross stirred first. "So, Kach Khanna is the same then," he said, cocking his head to the side, making Lexi's heart skip a beat.

"I do remember these little monsters." Lexi smacked her arm. "Vampires." Lexi heard a familiar buzz and swatted a mosquito making a meal out of her leg. Ross laughed and sang a made up song, "The mosquitoes of summer. Blood suckers"

She stood and, this time, extended her hand to Ross who took it.

He reached into his pocket. "I have something for that. It's pine sap. Keeps the bite from itching. The salve has natural antibiotics."

"That's clever." She pulled him into a hug before saying the first thing that came into her head. "Teach me to ride."

"Sure." Ross grinned. "You've changed your tune?"

Lexi asked him to explain. He said, "When we were little, you and Dot sat on the sidewalk watching the boys race go-karts. I never understood why you didn't want to try it."

"I think I was trying to blend into the background. I missed out on so much fun." Lexi smiled. "Let's hit the road before it starts raining harder. I may be more adventurous and braver now, but I'm not stupid. I want to get a lesson in before it starts pouring."

They walked to the bike at the entrance to the lake. Ross said, "Did you find what you were looking for? Coming back."

Lexi squeezed his hand. "I've been looking for a family since leaving here. I did find one. She leaned in and kissed him. His lips were soft and dry.

This time of year it would stay light until very late. Before this trip to Ward Lake, she hadn't been on a motorcycle since Jerry, but this was different. She knew Jerry for such a short time. It was an intense, emotion-packed relationship but ended with his disappearance and death.

With Ross, they had known each other since kindergarten. There were no nerves or guessing. He guided her to the seat in front of him and curved his body around hers, his hands resting on top of hers on the handlebars as they both pulled the clutch to shift gears. Ross let it out slowly and they rode away from the lake to the dirt road. She loved it. The freedom. The wind on her face. Her curly hair a tangled mess. She stopped the bike, twisted her hair into a knot and tucked it into the back of her jacket.

It was a heavy bike, but once Lexi felt comfortable stopping and starting on the dirt road, they took to the highway. She drove them back to town as the sun sank in the sky. They rode on familiar streets through town with fresh eyes.

Lexi admired how beautiful and wild Ketchikan remained. The thick forest covering Deer Mountain. The colors of the houses along Creek Street; the pink and green paint reflected in the creek at high tide on a rare sunny day. The wooden street on timber stilts that wound around the hill along the bank of Ketchikan Creek. The painted wooden salmon that seemed to rest unanchored to a rocky outcropping.

And rain. How much she loved to feel it on her skin. To let it soak her hair and face.

23

Lexi tries to understand the illicit drug market and how Johnny got involved; and, while updating Bob about the Sylvesters, hears a more in depth explanation of the saga.

Lexi sat in Bob's office. "How were drugs getting into Alaska when my parents were flying? Brody used to rant about how the hippies brought drugs up here in the 60s."

Bob sighed. "It has to do with warrantless seizures of luggage. They use sniffer dogs. It's complicated but the bottom line is you can't just look at a guy wearing bell bottoms and search his bags anymore.

"Did you know Johnny smuggled drugs onto my folks' plane?"

"I did." Bob leaned forward. "Wait, do you think Johnny had something to do with the crash?"

"I don't. And please don't say anything to Margaret. She knows about it but swears it was one time and he never did it again. But it was around the time the Sylvester family was stranded."

"Already two good ledes." Bob said, impressed. "I'll make a reporter of you yet. Listen, you are old enough to hear this and, if you really think your parents did not die in an accident, it could be another avenue."

Lexi took a pad of paper from her backpack and readied herself to take notes.

"Remember I told you June broke a huge story about Mayor Shasta? Well I didn't tell you everything. I still think of you as a kid, but I have to admit," he said with a hint of melancholy, "you are all grown up now. June was chasing a story about Mayor Shasta who was suspected of trafficking in child pornography."

Lexi gasped.

"His secretary told June she saw a picture in a drawer in his office. She raised the issue with him but quit after the mayor accused her of lying and made her doubt what she saw. It was a 'he said she said.' That's where the story ended, until–"

Bob stopped.

"Mayor Shasta's home caught fire and guess who was on the scene digging through the rubble?" He didn't pause for an answer. "Your mother–" Bob interrupted himself. "And guess what she found? There they were. Hundreds of pictures, most of them burned beyond recognition but there was enough evidence to convict him."

Bob paused again.

"Here's the interesting bit when it comes to June's plane. We were going to put the story out just before the accident. Everything came to a standstill when we lost Terry and June." Bob went quiet.

"We published a month later with my byline but it was your mother who broke the story."

Lexi put down her pencil, speechless.

Recovering, Bob said, "There was no evidence that the plane was tampered with and, honestly, I think Ruby Sylvester is a more likely person if there was any funny business going on."

Lexi explained to Bob that she had met Ruby and even taken a plane ride to Jim's Lake.

"You are very much like your mother, Lexi," said Bob, sounding impressed.

Bob said, "There's something you need to know about what happened to the Sylvesters. In the late 1950s, the Sylvester family, this time the entire family including the mother, went fishing and hunting on Coronation Island just off the coast of Prince of Whales Island. It's remote and dangerous but you can fish and hunt there. Once they boarded the plane, the weather shifted and Terry told them he couldn't safely get them to the island, but Mr. Sylvester insisted. Terry managed to get them to Coronation, but warned them that it was foolish. See, the father was a survivalist. He was teaching them how to live off the land."

Lexi turned the page of her notebook and started writing again.

"Your father should have insisted they cancel the trip, but he was skint at the time. His business was just getting off the ground."

Lexi felt embarrassed for her father.

Bob told Lexi that Mr. Sylvester booked a charter to drop them on a Friday and pick them up at the same location on Monday.

"But, on Monday–"

Lexi said quietly, "Another storm."

"Not just a storm," Bob said with a dramatic flourish of his hands, "a thunderstorm. Not super common around here but your father made the pick up and got everyone home safe."

"So they felt he could do it again." Lexi said.

"Exactly." Bob shook his head. "You have to remember in the 50s and even into the 60s it was a free for all up here. There were a lot of young men coming to the last frontier not knowing anything about the outdoors. Your dad was a daredevil. He thought nothing could touch him."

24

Long summer light means long summer evenings. Lexi ends the day talking murder with Carl and Felix. Cocktails flow as they construct a murder board and build a case around the idea that The Little Blackbird had been sabotaged, but by whom?

That evening after dinner, Lexi found herself at Carl and Felix's apartment swinging from a basket chair that hung from the ceiling by a chain. It was late into the night as the light faded and the twinkle lights around the windows became the only light in the room. Lexi kicked off her shoes.

"When did Alaska get to be so gay?" she asked.

Carl said, "All these lumberjacks, please. You weren't looking for it."

They settled in as Lexi told them about her harrowing flight with Ruby Sylvester.

Carl handed Lexi a drink. "If she was going to exact more revenge, that would have been the time."

They spent the next few minutes deciphering June's code from her journal. Carl figured it out almost immediately. June referred to an "R" but also to a set of numbers associated with meetings or liaisons. Carl explained that it was a simple alphabet code, numbers-to-letters. "A" equals "1" and so forth.

"18, 5, 25 is Rey and 15, 24, 5, 14 and 19 is Owens."

"So she didn't want anyone to know she was seeing Rey," said Lexi. "That makes sense. She *was* dating my father at the same time."

"Who is Rey Owens?" Felix asked from the kitchen where he was mixing a fresh batch of drinks. Lexi explained that Rey was a whale expert who, the journal confirmed, was seeing Lexi's mother.

Felix was impressed.

Carl approached the cork board on the wall next to Lexi. "What's with the spelling: Shouldn't it be

R A Y?" At the top of the Board was a hand-painted sign that read "MURDER BOARD." Carl switched on a string of lights he jerry rigged above the corkboard. Along with the twinkle lights, it gave the room a festive feel which seemed to Lexi the wrong mood for talk of murder, yet it was appropriate for the Rouge Arms and for their tipsy mood.

At the top of the murder board were index cards with Terry Fagan and June Fagan written on them. Tacked underneath, were yellowed photos cut out of newspapers and black and white photocopies Lexi found in the trunk in the attic or in Bob's office files, including the $5,000 check.

Carl said, "Well, that's interesting. Big oil giving Bob a check."

"A measly little five thousand." Felix took a drink and feigned disgust. "Hardly worth mentioning."

"I want a murder board for everything in my life." They laughed, stepping back to look at their handiwork.

From right to left was a photo of Ruby Sylvester, underneath was a sheet of paper with "family lost on Admiralty Island / blamed Terry" written on it. Next to that was written "Johnny" with "smuggled drugs onto the Beaver / covering his crime?"

Underneath the suspects names and Ruby's photo, were pictures of the Coast Guard photos of the crash and a few pieces of the plane that had been recovered.

Colette's cousin in the Coast Guard dropped off the report from Admiralty Island and from her parents plane crash to Carl before Lexi arrived.

"They must be very slow this time of year," Lexi said. "I only asked Collette this afternoon."

"We have something like 8,000 people in this tiny fishing village. It's not that busy. Have you read the crime blotter? Drunk and disorderlies. Besides," Carl said, stretching like a cat, "Collette lives at the Rouge Arms, second floor, 5B. She and her cousin were having dinner tonight."

Lexi brought the conversation back to the board. She told them the story Bob relayed about her father being a daredevil who rescued the family once before.

"Ruby is angry and extremely hurt but that's understandable. She lost most of her family in one day. I don't know what that's like." Carl started to protest but Lexi interrupted him. "I really don't. I basically never met my parents and, since no one talked about them, I was a selfish kid who only cared about myself and my friends. I didn't ask when I got old enough and should have cared. So right now is the first time I'm hearing almost too much about them. It's not unreasonable for Ruby to blame a person, and not the weather, or her father's judgment. I mean, why did he take her brother out on a raft during a storm?"

Carl interjected, "He was a survivalist but didn't seem to know much about survival."

Lexi put her foot on the floor to stop swinging. "Maybe that's what I'm doing here? Trying to place blame when it was an accident."

Carl was having none of it. "Darling. That is b.s. Before you start saying our murder board is a waste of time, let's look at the reports." Carl handed the Coast Guard Admiralty Island papers to Lexi who was grateful not to be reading about the plane crash. Then, Carl opened the report on her parents de Havilland DHC-2 Beaver accident and started to read.

He skimmed the pages murmuring "blah de blah" before landing on something interesting and stopped. "This confirms what Margaret told you." He looked up at Lexi. "It wasn't even raining the night your parents plane went down. But it does list 'pilot error' as the only explanation without giving one."

Lexi sat very still for a moment before picking up the pages she was holding. She flipped through until she found what she had been looking for in the Coast Guard report. "Here it is. It says here that there was a history-making storm and Terry had no choice but to land and ride it out. He radioed the Coast Guard that there were people on the island. It even cites his call to Margaret telling her the same thing." Carl squeezed into the hanging basket with Lexi.

"I guess that means we are back to the murder board," said Felix, getting up and announcing he would refresh everyone's drinks. On the way to the kitchen he leaned close to Lexi and said, "Your mother, what a dark horse. Rey Owens."

"Could she have sabotaged a plane?" Lexi asked. "But why would she? She studies whales."

"And who is the mysterious other 'RF?'" Carl added. "Apparently, June Fagan was irresistible."

Lexi felt defensive on her mother's behalf. "It could be a source she was meeting about a story for the paper?"

"Good point." Taking the proffered drink from Felix, Carl said, "I think Ruby Sylvester is more likely to have exacted revenge. What did your detective say? She had a motive. I agree, Lexi, what was Rey's motive? Having affairs with gay-curious straight women is common from what I know of the lesbians."

Lexi laughed. "I have a hard time believing my mother was having multiple affairs let alone one with Rey and possibly some mysterious "R" *and* my dad—even if it was the swinging 60s." She sipped her drink contemplatively before remembering to tell them about the professor.

"I met Sam Parker, the professor doing environmental studies that were just cover for the oil companies to point to if they were questioned about the impact of their drilling. She likes women too."

"Room for speculation there," he said, winking at Felix.

"I know one thing," Lexi said ignoring Carl. "Ruby may have had motive but she did not have opportunity. She was in Fairbanks at school. I called and the school confirmed the date."

Lexi kicked off of the ground and lifted her legs as the chair swung. Feeling the alcohol go to her head, she said, "I could not be investigating anything without the bat phone in your dad's office. I couldn't afford it." Struggling to get off the swing, Lexi walked to the murder board. She moved Ruby's picture to the side. Felix and Carl joined her.

"Do you have a photo of Rey Owens?" Carl asked.

"I do, but I don't think she would hurt June. She adored her."

"Some detective you are," he teased.

Lexi, sheepish, opened her book bag and took out Rey's book, handing it to Carl.

"You have her book!" He ran to get scissors and quickly cut out the author's photo from the back cover, tacking it up to the board where Ruby's photo had been.

Felix handed Lexi a shot glass with three layers of liquid. At the bottom was a dark ring of alcohol, the middle was a light caramel, and the top a light orange. She took a sip. "That is disgusting! What is it?"

"Whisky on top, Irish cream in the middle, and Kahlúa at the base. We call it the Duck Fart. Invented by a bored bartender in some hole-in-the-wall somewhere north. Wish I'd thought of it. Felix did a story about it at the radio station." Perplexed, Lexi frowned.

"Felix used to be a DJ at the local radio station. I bet you don't know who else has his own show?" He looked at Lexi who stared back at him.

"Ross," he said, triumphant.

"Why would I care about that?" Lexi asked grinning broadly.

"Pul-eeze!" Felix said, mocking her.

Carl raised his glass. "Now down in one." He took the shot. "It's all the rage," he croaked, his voice sounding as if he'd just smoked a pack of cigarettes. Lexi and Carl followed suit, coughing and laughing before bringing their attention back to the board.

"We're missing something," Lexi said as she stared at the photos. We moved Rey to 'suspects?' I just don't see her caring about Terry. He didn't seem to be an issue for her."

25

Lexi hears the hurtful truth—that the Native Alaskans were writing their own history while taking back what had always been theirs. Another trip to the library is followed by a traditional Potlatch ceremony with Ross.

The next day, Saturday, was foggy, the kind of weather that would make Lexi's hair an unholy halo. She wrapped her hair into a knot at the base of her neck and made her way to the kitchen.

She was on a mission to find the manual to the Beaver and look for clues on how someone might sabotage the plane. Where else would she look but the library.

She walked down the Edmonds Street stairs into town. Everything was wet. She stopped to admire a banana slug on the wooden railing. Now that Lexi had distance from her childhood, she realized it was a good place to grow up, if you took away the orphan part.

There was the abandoned playground just steps away from her front door, hilly streets to ride bikes down, hands free and legs splayed as the bike picked up speed. It was the kind of place where a split in a tree branch was turned into a treehouse and fallen trees covered with leafy branches easily became a fort.

On hot summer nights, when the light faded well past everyone's normal bedtimes, Lexi would sneak out of her bedroom window and crawl under the house along the wooden planks left to rot. She made her way, avoiding the rusty nails, to meet her friends. It was unsupervised fun. A wild bunch of neighborhood kids roaming the empty wet streets until someone's parents were heard calling for their child to come home to pleas of "It's not dark yet!" Everyone would scatter, grateful they were not the ones caught because it was, finally and definitely, dark.

Since it was the weekend, Lexi was not surprised to see Carl, Ross, Collette and Dot sitting on a boulder near the back entrance to the Old Hospital. They waved for her to join them.

Dot was saying, "Remember the Go-Cart races?"

Colette chimed in: "And the time we got locked in that creepy operating room."

"You were so scared," said Lexi as they all looked at Ross who threw his head back and laughed.

"Carl," Ross pointed at his friend still laughing, "you found an old surgery what-cha-ma-call-it and pretended to be possessed. You rat bastard."

"Nah mang." Carl shrugged his shoulders. "I don't remember that."

"If I'm lyin' I'm dyin'." Dot used an expression they had all overused when they were kids. Lexi laughed until her stomach hurt.

The area where Lexi grew up not only had an old hospital loosely converted to apartments, but an abandoned school with broken windows, a rusty seesaw, and a lopsided merry-go-round. The broken asphalt of the playground was used as a parking lot for the houses on Edmond Street.

When she was eight, Lexi picked up a rock and threw it at one of the windows of the abandoned school. She missed the window but Brody, who was rarely outside, saw her. She heard him yell, "Alexandra!" and her heart sank. Thinking about it now, she could not imagine why she picked up that rock. It took Brody a long time to forgive her and even longer to forgive herself.

Back at the rock, Colette told them she would return in a sec and ran into the building. Lexi and Dot awkwardly stuck up a conversation.

Colette emerged from the building a few minutes later holding an old transistor radio, the same one they had listened to as kids on summer evenings. Lexi pictured the gang sitting in this spot, teenagers eating beef jerky, spitting out sunflower seed shells, singing to the radio.

Turning the radio on, they heard an old Herb Alpert song they recognized. "This guy's in love with you. Yes I'm in love," they sang along. Lexi looked at Ross and blushed as they acted out the words. "My hands are shakin'. Don't let my heart keep breakin'." And for the final verse they each took a turn at plunging an imaginary dagger into their chests. "If not I'll just die-ey-ey." They fell over each other choking with laughter.

Lexi looked at her friends as they sang on this warm summer afternoon and thought how nice it was not to talk about her parents and what might have happened to them.

Dot turned to Lexi and asked, "Remember how your grandparents used flashlights instead of lamps next to their beds?"

"Never trust an old Catholic to understand convenience or even comfort." Lexi lowered her voice theatrically. "Doris put it in a drawer even though it just needed new batteries."

"No!" Dot said not believing her.

"If I'm lyin' I'm dyin'."

The transistor radio played "A, B, C" by the Jackson 5, high and tinny. Dot started singing "A", the rest followed suit, "B." Colette's clear soprano sang the "C. It's easy as one, two, three—" joined by Carl in his lovely tenor. They danced on the rock trying not to fall off the mossy surface, members of a motley choir.

Lexi was sorry she had to leave, but wanted to get to the library before it closed. It had been years since she had a weekend free since picking up shifts at McCracken's Bakery; though it was a way to see her friends who were everyday customers.

Ross was telling Dot how he was learning to repair damaged totem poles at the state park, Saxman Bight.

"When did you start carving?" Lexi asked.

"I carve, too," said Dot with pride.

"You both carve? For how long?"

Lexi's question was met with silence. "How did I not know that?"

"You never asked," Dot said bitterly.

Lexi flinched. She stared at Dot before saying, "Still. I should have known."

Dot looked at her, a sadness in her eyes.

Lexi tried to defend herself. "I wanted to figure out who I am away from home."

Dot looked at the ground. "Says the person who abandons her friends."

26

Lexi stops by the library and is shown where the stolen Eagle feather headdress once rested. She also discovers, to her shock, who checked out the manual for her parents' plane, which lead her back to where she had started.

Lexi waved at her grandmother, who was saying goodbye to the latest group of museum tourists, before asking the librarian if they carried manuals for seaplanes.

She approached Sandra, who even as high schoolers, everyone called Mrs. Andersson. She looked up from her book and smiled.

"Alexandra! Looking for Doris?" she teased.

"Not today," Lexi scoffed. "She's tortured her last tourist and headed for home. She and Kak have been wading through Brody's books." She checked her watch. 4:32pm. "Well, in an hour, it'll be high balls on the deck."

Mrs. Andersson asked, "What can I do you for?"

"Would you have any mechanical manuals for seaplanes?"

"Of course we do!" she said with enthusiasm. "We have one for the Beaver, the Little Blackbird, the Fagan floatplane. Margaret didn't need it but I ordered it nonetheless. Up here you have to fix what's broken, but wait." Sandra stood. "Didn't you hear we've been burgled?" She didn't stop for Lexi to answer, striding toward the museum indicating Lexi was to follow.

"This is where the Eagle feather headdress used to be, remember?" Lexi wondered why people thought she would forget something she had seen hundreds of times. Had she been gone that long?

They approached a large, glass case. The lock had been jimmied, the outline of the headdress pressed into the red velvet lining along the bottom. Mrs. Andersson lifted the glass and let Lexi trace the outline of the feathers with her hand. She could picture it clearly: large eagle feathers sewn into a thick beaded headband for the crown. Streamers of red felt, leather, feathers, and large beads flowed down the sides secured by a round beaded medallion.

"It wasn't even a Haida or Tlingit headdress," Mrs. Andersson said, staring into the empty space. "It was probably a Lakota or Comanche ceremonial piece. Sacred." She shook her head in disgust. "I hope it finds its way back to its people."

Lexi was thinking of how her Indian friends worked hard to keep a connection to their past, their ancestors, and how quickly she had walked away from hers. She also knew who had taken it and that it had returned to its home, but said, "Me, too."

Mrs. Andersson closed the case and they walked down the hall to the library part of the building leading Lexi to a shelf of manuals. A neat pile of thin books that looked as if they had not been touched for years. Mrs. Andersson pulled out a few and placed them on a nearby table. She shuffled through them.

"That's curious," she said absently. "I don't see it. Let me check the cards."

They walked back to the front where Mrs. Andersson opened the small drawer in the card catalog and flipped through the cards. She pulled one out. "Here it is." She peered at the card through the bottom of her bifocals. "I'll be darned. Look at that." She handed it to Lexi.

"The last person to check it out was Johnny Graham in 1965."

27

Lexi pushes Doris to clear clutter from the house that, unsurprisingly, turns out to be a mistake. At the newspaper office, she finds the manual that had been checked out to Johnny and freaks out before Bob tries to explain.

The next morning, Lexi found Doris looking out the window cradling her coffee. She wanted to find Margaret and ask about why Johnny would have checked out a manual for the Beaver, but first she needed to have a heart-to-heart with Doris.

"Gram," Lexi's voice was soft. "Should we tidy up? Get rid of Brody's chair and rearrange the front room?"

"No," Doris said, physically upset. "I'm not erasing your grandfather." She leaned on the back of a chair as Lexi protested that she had only suggested donating a very old, worn out chair.

"It has more to do with me than him." Doris gave her a reassuring smile. "When you're my age, change is not your friend. My eyes aren't what they used to be. If I move furniture, I'm likely to trip and falling is the death knell for the old. Best to keep the furniture the same and just tidy away your grandfather's detritus. Kak and I got rid of clothes and surface things–a declutter kind of thing. Otherwise, I'd be looking for Brody and brooding." Doris gestured toward Brody's chair. "Moving furniture would be like living with landmines."

Considering that Lexi had worked in an old folks' home, it had not occurred to her that they never moved the furniture. She thought about her friend Henry's apartment and how everything had seemed set in place for the last 50-odd-years. She, again, regretted leaving Saxman with him. His eyesight was poor, but he sounded happy for the company when she suggested it. But, what if he tripped over her? Before she headed back to San Francisco, she would make one final call on the bat phone to check up on Henry and Saxman.

She downed a weak cup of coffee before heading first to the newspaper office and then to track down Margaret.

Bob was on the phone and waved her to the back of the building to do whatever research needed to get done.

There were stacks of papers, flyers for events from years past, even an old scrap of bear fur and a ripped piece of traditional Haida ceremonial garb, a button blanket, the shell still shining on the red felt. She moved the pile aside and saw what looked like a dog eared pamphlet and picked it up. The cover was a hand-drawn seaplane. It was a beat up plane manual.

She read the cover out loud: "de Havilland Canada DHC-2 Beaver Floatplane." She ran into the front office where Bob Kincaid was banging out a story on his typewriter.

"Bob!" she shouted, showing him the manual. "Why do you have this?"

Bob looked up from the typewriter. It took him a few seconds to recognize what she was holding.

"Will you look at that," he reached for the book and opened the pages. "Man. I haven't seen this in years. Must have been for the story about the accident."

He stared at the pages. "As heartbreaking as it was, I had to write about what happened. This is a newspaper." He explained that he wrote stories before the accident about her parents and their charter business. "It's not every day you hear about lady bush pilots." He smiled and handed the manual back to Lexi. "I really need to clean that back office and return it to the library."

Lexi stood her ground. "Why did Johnny check it out of the library 22 years ago?"

Bob looked confused.

"1965. The year the plane went down."

"Of course," Bob said calmly. "I was writing about the crash. I needed details for the story. I'm sure he or I had checked it out before that, too. Johnny did odd jobs for me and I asked him to check it out. Margaret was too broken up for me to ask what she knew about the plane and what would happen when it crashed."

Lexi was embarrassed. She had taken what Margaret had said at Kak's to heart, that the plane must have been sabotaged. Again she felt as if she were on the wrong track and that maybe thinking it was not an accident was a way for Margaret to cope.

If they never figured out what happened Margaret would always think she had missed something and somehow caused the plane to crash and her best friends to die.

"Listen, if it will make you feel any better," Bob paused to write down some dates. "Look at

October 20th or 21st 1965—that week—and you'll see the articles I wrote about the accident."

Bob looked at Lexi with what seemed like pity. "This is going to be painful for you, but for the next few years I did follow ups so check October 19th '66 and '67. It will be easier for you to look up old newspapers at the library. You see what a mess it is here. Maybe reading about it will bring you some peace. Or not, you can just let it go, Alexandra."

She took the scrap of paper Bob offered her.

"I started to think there was a reason Doris and Brody never talked about their own daughter."

Bob sighed. "It's that generation. They lived through the Depression and the war. They don't talk about anything. It's like pulling teeth trying to interview old people sometimes. They are not the most self-reflective generation."

"When I worked at the Pioneer Home, the residents loved to talk. Maybe they were just lonely."

"I bet they mostly talked about their families and never about the war."

Lexi nodded.

"You're a grown woman now." Bob came round the desk and walked her to the front door. "Start asking around about Terry and June. It's a small town. You'll find plenty of folks to talk to. Now head. I have a newspaper to put out for tomorrow."

Before he closed the door, he said with gusto, "That should be our motto: Yesterday's news today."

Lexi walked to Grant Street and turned toward Deer Mountain. Her mind was racing. She was not ready to give up yet; though she had a well-rehearsed fantasy about her parents, the idea of bringing them back down to earth was painful. There was her mother's infidelity. Conflicting information about her father. Did he fly when he had been drinking? No matter what, she had to find out what really happened the day of the crash, even if it turned out to be pilot error on a cloudless day like today.

Clearly, coming home had dredged up wounds and not just from the distant past. There were things Lexi needed to resolve, like Dot's feeling that she had been dropped as a friend when Lexi left, and she was probably not the only one.

Lexi and Ross had a date to meet up. There was no place private since Ross moved back in with his family after college to save money for his own place. He was teaching but hoping to get a job with the Prudhoe Bay Oil Fields at the northern tip of the state.

"It's tough work but after a few years, you have a nest egg and I could come home and help my family with the fishing business. My dad makes money carving but demand goes in waves."

Ross was sitting on his twin bed, Lexi next to him.

"The oil company doesn't hire a lot of natives." They hire their own but, as he told Lexi, he had a shot because his uncle worked there and he was trying to get some native kids on the crews. Lexi had never been in Ross's room before. They weren't that close as kids. He hung out with his cousins by the time they were in high school.

"You know, I always wanted to know you better." Ross said.

"You did?" Lexi asked. "You know, I didn't realize how much of my life I put on hold because of my parents. The only people who mentioned my dead parents were the bullies who teased me. Doris and Brody hardly mentioned my mother and never talked about my dad."

"I can understand it," Ross said, putting his arm around her shoulders. "It's traumatic to lose people so near to you. It shuts some people down.

Look at my Uncle Johnny." He brushed a curl from Lexi's forehead. "You were actually a fun kid."

She hugged him as hard as she could trying not to cry. Once she released him, Ross said, "Until you started working in the old folks home and smelled of oatmeal and spoiled milk." They laughed.

They talked about their 6th grade graduation trip to Refuge Cove where the Principal, Sister Mary Raymond, bludgeoned a rock fish to death with a bat that had a nail embedded on its tip.

"Total carnage!" Ross laughed.

"Terrifying." Lexi agreed. "Remember how we just stared at the bloody fish mangled on the bottom of the boat?"

"Why did she pick us for that horror film of a fishing trip? We would have been happy frying eggs on a rock with the rest of the class."

"We were quiet kids. Maybe Sister Mary Raymond thought we were praying over that dead fish. What a joke."

Lexi looked around the room. There was a poster of the Brazilian soccer star Pelé behind the bed and a Star Wars poster on the opposite wall. Lexi had the same poster of Luke and Princess Leia in her room during high school.

"You haven't changed your room since you were a kid?" She said, smiling at Ross.

Ross leaned into her. "I still love the things I did then." He lifted her face and kissed her. They fell onto the bed, entwined.

28

Lexi spends another afternoon in a bar with friends and is schooled by another former teacher on the nature of teaching teenagers.

The night before, Lexi got a call from Carl to meet her friends at The Pioneer Bar for "Sunday church" as he called it. Lexi mused that bars in her home town were like coffee shops in San Francisco, one on every corner.

Restless at home, Lexi arrived early. She saw Johnny sitting at the bar and asked to join him.

He pointed to his glass. "This is water. Ask Mary."

Lexi told him there was no need, though Mary nodded a confirmation as she walked over. Lexi was surprised to see Mary behind the bar, this was not the Frontier Bar, where Mary had worked as long as Lexi could remember.

She said, "Moonlighting I see."

"Yeah, yeah." Mary took the towel from her shoulder and polished a glass. "More like day lighting. It's so early. Water for you, too?"

"You choose," Lexi said. "You've known me since I was a kid. Give me something delicious."

Lexi turned to Johnny. After a little chit chat, she looked him dead in the eye and said, "I know you smuggled drugs on The Little Blackbird."

To her surprise, he fell apart. "I promise it was only a few times," he pleaded. "Margaret found out and that was it. I don't even know who was supposed to pick up the packages." He shook his head. "Man, for all I know the pot could still be in the plane."

Lexi was inclined to believe him, not the part about the pot not getting picked up, but that he was just a courier. He was a lot of things, but a hardened criminal was not one of them.

Mary placed a pink drink on the bar. "It's about time you had a real drink after all those years of Shirley Temples."

Lexi took a sip. It was better without alcohol but she was game to keep drinking. Once Mary disappeared in the back, Johnny said, "Look at Professor Parker. She was knee deep in smuggling."

"Samantha?"

"You know her?"

"I met her and asked about chartering the plane for her oil company, while doing bogus environmental studies."

Johnny scoffed. "Is that what she told you?"

Lexi asked what he knew.

"At least she admitted that her work was hogwash. We're nowhere near where the pipeline was eventually built. It runs closer to the Canadian border and stops at Valdez. If you were doing any work connected to the pipeline you'd fly out of Anchorage."

Lexi was perplexed. She remembered an article she read in the archives. They struck oil at the tip of Alaska where the land meets the Arctic Ocean in Prudhoe Bay in 1968. Her parents' plane went down in 1965.

"But the pipeline hadn't been built yet." Lexi protested. "How would they know where it would go or even if they would find oil?"

Johnny smiled slyly. "Right, they hadn't even discovered oil yet. It was the great exploration. That was the point. Parker was supposed to be finding the best place to run the pipeline because they were sure there was oil up here somewhere and they wanted the easiest route with the lowest environmental impact. Or at least they wanted it to appear that they cared about the impact on the land and the people."

"It doesn't make sense. If they hadn't discovered oil yet, why pay someone to look for a place for a pipeline?"

"You'll have to ask her. What she was really doing on the oil company's dime was delivering drugs to remote communities, not that your folks knew anything about it. She was the courier." He sat up. "You're the first person I ever told that to. Margaret only knew that I smuggled pot on the plane a couple of times and that it was for some remote fishing crew. I could easily put the dime bags into one of the boxes already on the plane. I was at the hangar a lot in those days. It was a busy time." He added quickly, "Margaret doesn't know anything about Professor Parker."

"How do you know about Parker and the drugs?"

"That was a very small world. It was hush hush but those that knew, knew."

They sat in silence for a few minutes. Lexi continued to believe him but could think of no reason for professor Parker to want to kill her parents. They clearly did not know about the drug smuggling, no one did except Margaret, who only knew part of the story and wanted to protect Johnny, but Lexi refused to believe that it was at the cost of her parents' lives.

The alcohol version of a Shirley Temple was going to Lexi's head. She blurted out: "Why did you check out the plane's manual from the library?"

"I didn't need the manual; planes are Margaret's department. I got it for Bob. He needed to write a story about the crash. He had to describe what parts of the plane were missing." Johnny frowned at Lexi.

She gave him a reassuring smile to show it was okay to talk about it.

Johnny fidgeted in his seat. "Once, and only once–it was a small amount of cocaine–we aren't talking about a drug cartel here. I promise you." Johnny pleaded. "Samantha–professor Parker–gave me a rucksack, I stowed it on the plane and a guy at the landing spot was supposed to retrieve it when the cargo was being unloaded along with the medical supplies. This would be early '65. My memory is not good."

"Listen," he looked as if he wanted a drink, but took a gulp of his water. "You're too young to know this, but, back then, the cops could go through anyone's bags at the airport and ferry docks at any time. They rifled through every bag that came into Alaska to keep drugs out and it worked. After the case, Ohio versus something in '68." He stopped to think. "I wonder if it was a coincidence that they found oil that year?"

Lexi waited for him to continue.

"After that, the cop had to have a reason to search your stuff. Before that, it was the usual cowboys and Indians. The cowboys, the cops, always won."

Lexi looked surprised. Johnny clarified, "I was studying to be a lawyer before things got hairy. So there were no drugs in Alaska. That's why it was such a small operation that ended when your folks died."

Lexi was floored.

"Samantha was on the make." Johnny was staring into his empty glass. "She had a habit to support so agreed to be the courier. And working for the oil companies was a good cover."

Mary poured him another glass of water.

"I was really messed up. It's not an excuse, but I was blind drunk most of the time. Margaret never gave up on me. And I've given up the weed." He smiled sheepishly. "Promise."

Lexi saw Dot, Carl, and Ross walk in and sit at a table near the window. She thanked Johnny, who nodded.

She put on a smile and set her drink on the table before sitting down with her friends.

Carl said, "Looks like you've already been to communion. What is that 'I just confessed my sins' smile?"

Lexi laughed. "For my sins" she said, taking a sip of her pink concoction. Not wanting to talk about what she just learned, she steered the conversation toward work and the weather. Detective Reiger was right—digging up the past could be painful.

Lexi and Ross were not seated next to each other but their eyes were often on the other. They agreed not to tell anyone they were seeing each other. Carl suspected, of course, but the less he knew the better. Everyone would think Ross would get hurt, though Lexi's opinion was that it was more likely to be her heart that got broken.

No matter what, it was a relief for Lexi to be with her friends again. Getting up to use the bathroom she motioned for Dot to join her.

They smiled as they saw themselves reflected in the scratched up mirror, like a fun-house mirror that distorted their faces. Lexi looked at Dot's reflection, her face as lovely as ever. Her caramel skin glowing from the humidity, her black hair in short, loose braids.

Lexi blurted out. "I am so sorry I left like that."

"I was pretty hard on you." Dot nudged her with her shoulder.

Lexi nudged her back. "It was thoughtless." With renewed energy, Lexi accused Dot of not writing to her.

"I got one postcard without an address." Though her face was serious, there was a smile in Dot's voice. "Was I supposed to send a letter to 'Alexandra Fagan, San Francisco?'"

This sent them into fits of tipsy laughter. A woman walked into the bathroom and, for no reason, made them laugh even harder.

Lexi caught her breath and said, "Even if you've forgiven me, I promise to be better. I'll write more and you should visit."

"I might want to bring someone," Dot said casually.

Lexi raised an eyebrow.

"I'm seeing someone new." She gave Lexi the side eye. "Grace."

"Grace? Did we know her from school?" Lexi refused to be surprised.

"No." Dot re-applied lipstick in the mirror. "She moved here from Akhiok on Kodiak Island. To her, Ketchikan is the big city."

"Has she abandoned her Kodiak friends?" Lexi teased.

"As if," Dot said. "You know we couldn't do that if we wanted to but they don't have a post office so she's off the hook most of the time."

They fussed with their hair and walked back to the table knowing that rekindling their childhood closeness long-distance was a long shot but glad they were willing to try.

As soon as they sat down, the bar door opened flooding the room with light, and everyone at the table stopped talking and looked. A shadow appeared before materializing in the light – their high school history teacher.

Ross said, "Look, there's Mr. White." He looked much the same, a bit disheveled with a shaggy mustache.

Lexi got up, turned to her friends and said, "Let's go and talk to him." She walked to where Mr. White was sitting at the bar, turned around to look for her friends but saw they were still sitting staring at her. She gave them a "what the heck" look. They waved and went back to talking.

She turned to Mr. White and said, "Hi, remember me?"

"Alexandra Fagan. Of course I do. Your folks died in a plane crash." He stuck out his hand. "How the hell are you?"

If Lexi needed confirmation of how people saw her, there it was like a slap in the face.

Lexi still could not get used to teachers swearing. "I'm hella good. Mr. White—"

"Call me Darren. We're out of school."

"Darren? I just can't Mr. White."

Lexi was on the South side of tipsy and blurted, "This may seem like a strange question but why didn't we learn anything about Native culture in school?"

"Not you too." Mr. White seemed weary. "Listen, everything we failed to do–which is legit I admit–is going to be rectified. This state is the Saudi Arabia of the North. We are awash in oil money. Cultural centers are springing up everywhere. Ketchikan is ahead of the curve with potlatch ceremonies and two of the biggest totem parks in the world–that's world with a capital 'W' Alexandra. If you wanted to know anything Haida, Tlingit or even Eskimos for God's sake, you could have found it out."

Before she could reply, he continued. "But since you asked, here's the short version. I hate to sound hippy dippy but there was very little work for Natives 20 years ago. I studied Northwest Indian culture in graduate school in Seattle. I wrote a few papers," he said proudly.

Lexi held up her hand for him to pause, waved Mary over and ordered a coffee before motioning for Mr. White to continue.

He seemed primed for a lecture.

"For thousands of years, the Indians believed they were not separate from nature. The concept of dominating, exploiting, and just using resources to make someone rich, was just not there. It's not that they didn't like comfort or conveniences, but they fundamentally thought about nature as equals with them. As I understand it, they considered themselves guardians of the natural world, not apex predators. In the modern world, the white man's world, they lose because of prejudice and ignorance."

He took a drink. "But, don't romanticize them too much like the hippies do. There were richer tribes and many thought they were better than others. There was a hierarchy within the culture. The Tlingits even enslaved people from tribes they didn't consider to be high born—I'm using a Western term here but you get my meaning. They thought the Eskimos were inferior. A sense of superiority, not with nature, but with others, was not unknown in the ancient world."

Mr. White took a deep breath after his soliloquy.

Lexi was speechless. Taking her silence for wanting to hear more, Mr. White finished schooling her. "They were not the guardians of their fellow Indians, just guardians of nature, especially the Haida believed this, that they existed with nature not above it." A reckless grin appeared on his face that Lexi recognized from class. "Then again," he said triumphantly, "history was written by the white man."

Lexi said, "Mr. White!"

He was enjoying himself. "Yes, I live with the irony."

Lexi stood, drained her coffee, and implored him to join her friends. He picked up his martini and they walked to the table where his former students waited.

Lexi announced: "Mr. White Man is an Indian Expert."

They laughed.

"Truth be told," Mr. White said, holding his drink as if at a cocktail party. "When you were in my class, you kids didn't give a rat's ass about culture of any kind, let alone history. Too full of hormones." His face broke into a wide, genuine smile. "Listen, I love being a teacher. I even loved you ignorant, selfish, and self-centered mush-brains and, no doubt, I will enjoy trying to teach something to my students starting in the fall."

He turned to Lexi standing next to him, drained his glass, and said, "Now join your tribe. I'm headed home to mine." Mr. White gave a deep, slow bow and left the bar.

When they ate and sobered up, Lexi said goodbye to Ross, Dot and Grace before walking arm-in-arm with Carl and Felix to their apartment.

At the apartment, Lexi stood with her friends at the murder board which seemed to be expanding to include anyone her parents knew at the time of the crash. And, it was starting to look more professional.

The three columns from left to right were "SUSPECTS," "FRIENDS," and "ALIBIS." Johnny had been eliminated, his picture moved to the "ALIBI" column next to Margaret. The former Mayor, Richard Shasta, was in the suspects column along with two bush pilots that ran a competing business. The oil company shill, Professor Samantha Parker, was in the alibi column along with Ruby Sylvester who, at one time, was a prime suspect since she threatened Lexi's father and blamed him for the death of her family. Rey Owens was in the friends column. Felix had drawn a heart on her photo.

Carl went into the kitchen to make drinks. Felix scooted closer to Lexi and whispered, "Don't let Carl fool you. It's not easy being out here. You may have an anonymous encounter that turns into a beating when the man decides he likes it but hates himself for it."

"Boy was I drunk last night," Lexi quoted the film "Boys in the Band." Felix agreed.

Lexi put her arm around him before he continued. "And a few of my aunts are Christian and do not accept me. Luckily my parents adopted the old ways and love me for who I am." Felix glanced toward the kitchen. "Don't say anything to Carl. He enjoys being open in public, but I have to hide more. This is our safe haven."

"This is our Sunday evensong–evening prayers for the uninitiated," Carl said as he walked slowly out of the kitchen with two full martini glasses, handed one to Felix and the other to Lexi. "Be right back and we'll have a toast." Lexi never had this many drinks in a day, but she did not hate it. Between taking the varnish off her parents' image, the possibility they were murdered, and feeling like she had dumped her friends when she moved, there was a mix of happiness, relief, and dread. Drinking seemed appropriate under the circumstances.

Once they toasted, they got back to business and turned their attention to the cork board.

Felix took out a folder with freshly printed photographs. "I thought I would take a few snaps of anyone we've talked about. Those newspaper photos are too faded."

"Why do we have a 'FRIEND' category?" Felix said, defensively. "It doesn't even have anything under it." He tacked up a photo. "Here's one of Kak."

"Kak!" Lexi almost spilled her drink.

Carl placated Felix with "Good to cover all bases."

"At this rate everyone in town will be on the board." Lexi was only half kidding.

Felix pulled out of the small stack of photos of Bob.

Lexi said, "But Bob? Where's his motive?"

Rolling his "r's" Carl said "Rrrrrobert's on the big board" as he wrote Robert Kincaid at the bottom of the Polaroid.

29

Lexi catches up with Detective Reiger who has tracked down the young man, now grown, who ran over his daughter and killed her. As Lexi is well aware, knowing the truth does not always make it better.

In the Mayor's office on the magic phone, Lexi felt the weight of the receiver as Detective Reiger was telling Lexi, "I heard from a guy at the Oakland police looking into Jada's hit and run."

"Did he find something?"

"He did."

Lexi held her breath.

His voice was angry. "It was a guy - a kid really - joyriding." Detective Reiger collected himself as Lexi waited.

"I followed him." Reiger's voice was low. "Watched him with friends. At cafes with his family.

Lexi gasped. "He has kids?"

"He does. He's a defense lawyer. Works in the DA's office in Berkeley. I sat in the courtroom and watched him defend clients. I talked with his superiors. Then, a few weeks ago, he cornered me on the street. Told me he'd seen me following him and wanted to know what I was about."

"What did you say?"

Reiger went silent. Knowing he was a private person, Lexi wished she had not asked.

"Let's just say there was some anger involved."

Lexi understood Reiger. There is a rage that comes with a sudden and pointless death. She held her tongue, knowing he would tell the full story when he was ready.

Reiger closed his eyes, remembering the exchange. "And you know what he did?" Reiger surprised her by chuckling. "He hugged me. He threw his arms around me and bawled like a baby."

He took a deep breath. "I could feel the pain in him. The regret. There was even a sense of relief that he'd been found out. He had a hearing to get to so we agreed to meet for coffee to talk in a few days.

She said before thinking, "He's here and Jada should be here."

Reiger repeated in a whisper, "She should be here."

It felt like the silence stretched for a long time.

Eventually, Reiger said, recovering, "This call had better be free as you say."

Lexi had more questions but understood Reiger did not want to continue talking about it.

"How are you holding up?" He asked.

She answered: "I'm a bit discombobulated. Doris is holding up remarkably well. It was his time to go so that takes some of the sting out." Enough talk of death, Lexi changed the subject. "Are you checking up on my bakery friends?"

"As an excuse to stop by and get a bear claw on my way to work." He patted his belly. "It's a bad habit." Reiger leaned back in his chair, letting the fan send hot air across his face. "Stella grills me about cases I'm working on. Henry's there. I don't think the new girl gives him eclairs so he's eating donuts. Timm always manages to make his stories about the indignities of getting around on crutches funny."

"Do they think everyone who dies has been murdered?" Lexie asked.

"Of course." Reiger paused. "Don't tell me there's a body anywhere near you?"

She laughed, "No." Lexi started talking fast as she did when she didn't want to be told she had an overactive imagination, mostly around Reiger. "But I am hoping you can tell me how to tell if someone is telling you the truth."

"That's a 'telling' request." Reiger smiled. "Now slow down and *tell me* why you're asking?"

Lexi spilled the beans about everything she had heard so far—Margaret's suspicions about the plane going down and how she did not tell the authorities because of Johnny, that June might have married Terry because she was pregnant with her, and that June might have been having an affair with a woman. Lexi was not sure why she added that detail but she could not stop talking.

She told him that Margaret and the newspaper editor had been piecing together the plane, bit by found bit, all these years. About Professor Parker, oil exploration, the pipeline, drug running, her frightening flight with Ruby Sylvester and Ruby's grudge against Terry.

When Lexi was finished, there was only static on the line. She knew him well enough to know he was weighing everything she had told him.

"Nothing like a small town for ya," Reiger mused.

Lexi said, "You got it in one."

He took a long, clarifying breath and said, "Listen, if you really think there's a possibility that someone wanted to hurt your parents, you need evidence." After a short pause he said, "I keep saying it, but be careful."

"So you think there's something here?"

"I believe you believe there is something there. And I believe you. Go back to the beginning. Eliminate dead ends and dig deeper where you have questions. Go back over what you know and what you don't know. When you have a question, ask."

"I need to talk to Professor Parker again. How do I get her to tell me the truth?"

"Tell her what you heard. If she refuses to answer, that tells you something. If she admits or denies it, that also tells you something. Every reaction will get you closer to the truth. Watch her body language. Does she meet your eyes when she's talking? If she doesn't, she could be hiding something. A lot of it is paying close attention to the answer and how it's delivered."

Lexi thanked him. "That is a help."

Reiger glanced at the clock. It was nearly time for a status meeting on cases. "Listen, Lexi, I have to run." Before he rang off, he said with gravity. "Be safe."

They said their goodbyes and hung up. Lexi was stunned, almost to the point of shock, at how the ghosts of the past were clamoring for attention.

Back at home, Kak and Doris sat at the kitchen table. Doris got up to leave for the library but insisted Kak and Lexi stay put. Doris threw on her rain slicker and rubber boots and closed the door behind her.

"Get some coffee and sit." Kak patted the seat where her grandmother had been sitting. Lexi did as she was told. Sitting next to Kak, Lexi looked around the house and marveled at how they had donated, thrown away, and stored any sign of Brody but the furniture.

Kak was unusually thoughtful. "Lexi, you are running from something but not toward anything. What is going on with you?"

Lexi, who had always been a little intimidated by Kak, was taken aback. "What do you mean?"

"You forget, after my accident, I was a guidance counselor at White Cliff." Kak reminded Lexi that she had fallen from a tree during her lumberjack days and had to retire to a desk job at 45.

"I didn't go to White Cliff," Lexi said defensively.

"Maybe if you had you would have made something of yourself." Kak's remark landed hard.

"You know I love you, kid, so don't give me a gloomy face." Lexi thought that surely there was a compliment in there somewhere.

Kak took a drag of her cigarette letting the smoke drift slowly from her mouth. "It's time we started treating you like the adult you have become." Like all conversations with Kak, she turned it back to herself. "When I was at White Cliff, I was having an affair with your Middle School English teacher, Mr. LeBlanc, from Schoenbar."

Carl had told Lexi Mr. LaBlanc was straight but, at the time, the rumor was that he was not. "Didn't everyone think he was gay?"

"Well, if he was, there's three fourths of him that's gay, but I got the fourth that was curious and we had a moment in the 60s." She threw her head back and laughed. Lexi joined her. There was no defense against a conversation with Kak.

Lexi tried another tack. "Why are you telling me this?"

"My first husband, before Vincent, was the Principal at White Cliff. He fired me," Kak said unfazed. Lexi tried to read Kak's face. She might have been pulling her leg.

"In those days, you could fire anybody for anything. He found a pretext."

Lexi was confused. "That doesn't seem right? It was a different school."

"Honey, that's not the half of it." Kak took one last drag of her smoke before stabbing the butt into an ashtray. "It was before you were born but now you're a big girl and need to know that people have affairs."

"What people?" Lexi thought she was talking about Brody or Doris.

Kak said flatly. "Your parents."

Lexi was almost relieved. "I know my mother had an affair. Did my dad have an affair?"

"He was," Kak waved her hand dismissively, "with me."

Lexi was stunned. "What? You slept with my dad? That's why you were fired?"

"It's hard to keep secrets up here." Kak stood, abruptly. "You need to know who your parents were. But believe me it lasted a hot minute." She walked to the door and stepped into her galoshes. "By the time you were old enough to hear it, your grandparents wanted to spare you. Your dad was a dud, but your mother had a pull on people. She was–" Kak went silent as if searching for the word. "She had charisma." Grabbing her raincoat, she said, "It was all such a long time ago."

Before walking out of the front door, Kak turned and said over her shoulder, "I've wanted to tell you that for years. I'm glad that's over."

Lexi thought, for me, it's only the beginning.

The door closed behind Kak and the house was, again, silent.

30

Reiger meets the man who changed the trajectory of so many lives.

Reiger and Billy sat across from each other at the cafe near the U.C. Berkeley campus at Bancroft and Telegraph. It was crowded with plants hanging in beaded pot holders that streamed to the floor. Book shelves lined the walls crammed with dog-eared books donated by customers. Tables along the walls were stacked with leaflets and announcements. It was noisy with the chatter of students talking, TA's counseling, and a few dazed parents staring at these unfamiliar surroundings nursing cups of coffee.

Reiger looked the young man in the eye. "Tell me what happened."

Billy tried to talk but started weeping softly. Reiger stared at him stone faced. Eventually, Billy said, his voice a whisper, "I had been partying, drinking, and I was speeding and I swear I thought I clipped a car." A sob caught in his throat before he continued. "I didn't know until I heard the news later that it was–"

"My daughter, Jada." Reiger fought the tears that welled in him. "Keep talking, son."

Billy flinched at the way Reiger spoke to him. He was not angry. His voice was steady. Billy felt he did not deserve respectful treatment. He wanted Reiger to punch him, pummel him, punish him.

After a time, Billy said tentatively. "I went down a dark path after that. Drinking, losing jobs, friends. I told nobody about what happened, tried to numb away the pain of what I'd done. Erase my feelings." He choked on his words. Reiger put his hand on the young man's shoulder in an act of such compassion it nearly broke Billy.

"My mother begged me to go to church with her. And one day, I don't know why, I did."

The library had always been one of Lexi's happy places. It was where she now found herself sitting with her head in her hand. The library had always been her safe place, an escape to read about other places and other lives. It was quiet, unlike at home with the television blaring because Brody, and often Doris, did not wear their hearing aids at home, but now, when she was home, the house was quiet and she missed the television, the acrid smell of a pipe, her grandmother burning coffee Doris had forgotten was on the stove.

She had come for her grandfather's funeral and expected things had changed, but now discovered that she was the one who had changed.

Her friends in San Francisco thought being from a town in Alaska had defined her in funny ways. They teased her good naturedly about being a country bumpkin, naive and wide eyed.

Maybe it was time for her to figure out what it meant to be from Ketchikan. It could be that it was exotic, as her city friends thought, and that it was also provincial, as she often felt.

She sat in the section with books about Alaska. Calling it a section, thought Lexi, was generous since there were two books. She opened the first and read that Ketchikan had been the largest city in Alaska in the 1920s because of the salmon industry when canneries were still big business.

"By the early 1930s, there were over a dozen canneries along the waterfronts of the Southern Southeast region of which Ketchikan was the economic hub."

Lexi knew from growing up with the stench of the pulp mill that timber was the next economic engine. At the same time the city's natural resources were making a lot of people rich, the Native population had moved from their villages along the coast to the cities to look for work, but unlike the Chinese who were encouraged to move to the lower 48s to build railroads, the Native Alaskans were overlooked because of the young white men streaming into Alaska.

There were a few pages on the infamous Dolly's House, one of many houses on the wooden walkway at 24 Creek Street held up by pilings winding its way along a thicket of trees with Ketchikan Creek rushing below. A successful madam, Dolly Arthur's brothel remained open until the 50s.

Lexi read with amusement that the trail she and her friends often took to a lookout on Deer Mountain was called Married Man's Trail after Dolly's customers who made quick exits every time the Red Light District was raided by police.

31

Detective Reiger and the truth about what happened to Jada.

Lexi was discovered by a secretary using the phone in the mayor's office but, to her surprise, the woman had been a friend of June's. She walked into the small room, gave Lexi a hug while she was on the phone with Detective Reiger, and winked at her as she closed the door behind her, leaving Lexi to her call.

Reiger was telling her how it went with the kid, now a man, who had killed his 12-year-old daughter, ran her over and took off on the streets of Oakland.

"But, ironically, he found God." Reiger scratched his beard.

"I took him out for coffee. We talked. He told me he'd been a punk in his youth. He was speeding and didn't see her. He was drunk and just kept driving. That he spiraled even further into depression and drugs after he heard about a young girl that died in a hit-and-run. He was in the wilderness of grief and guilt for years."

Lexi felt sick imagining it.

Reiger continued. "He told me that when he turned 30, he had a dream where the little girl he hit came to him and begged him to stop punishing himself. That his life did not have to be sacrificed for hers. She forgave him." Here Reiger's breath caught in his throat.

"After that day, he turned his life around. Started going to church with his mama. Went to law school. Married and had kids of his own. Always thinking that, someday, this day would come. I told him that I never thought this day would come for me. The day that I would lose my faith and want to kill another person for what he did to my Jada. But having watched him, followed him, seen his mother, his grandmother, his kids playing on the street just like Jada. I did not see a killer. I didn't see a heartless man who ran over a little girl, my child."

Lexi tamped down her grief and, knowing detective Reiger had deep faith, asked, "What now?"

There was a long pause. Reiger rubbed his forehead, his voice was deep with resolve. "I believe that God has forgiven him so how can I not forgive him?"

"I don't know that I could do that." Lexi moved the receiver to her other ear. "And Jackie?"

"She can't forgive him." Reiger continued, "but that is her way and her path."

32

Dot and Lexi have a fight, bury the hatchet, but not without a few nicks.

Still reeling from her call with detective Reiger, Lexi stopped by the corner market near Ketchikan Creek for a bottle of Coke when she noticed Dot standing at the open freezer.

Getting her attention, Lexi asked, "If you're free, mind if I stop by your place?"

To Lexi's surprise, Dot shrugged unenthusiastically.

They walked up the stairs to the Old Hospital in silence. The building looked as neglected as ever. Once inside Dot's apartment, Lexi looked around the cracked green paint. The bed against the wall, the hot plate under the small window with wires threaded through the dirty glass as if it were a prison and not a place that once healed people.

Dot offered tea and, before Lexi could accept, which she did, filled a pot with water and turned on the hot plate.

Turning to Lexi, Dot said, "You couldn't wait to leave." As if it were draining to say it, Dot almost collapsed onto her worn sofa. "You were out of here right after high school. You quit the old folks home and, poof! You were gone."

Lexi was taken aback. "Dot, you worked at the old folks home, too. You could have saved your money and left like I did."

They sat in awkward silence. Lexi sank into the couch next to Dot.

"And go where?" Dot's face had fallen. "Without my family, who am I?"

Lexi sighed, baffled by Dot's accusations. "That's the point. To find out who you are." She looked at Dot's face that was contorted with pain. "Why haven't you left? What is it really about?"

Dot was almost pleading. "I had my family to support. It's not easy for us to leave. It's our home." After a long pause, Dot said, "To be honest–" she hesitated, "it never occurred to me to leave."

This statement stunned Lexi. As long as she could remember, all she had ever thought about was leaving this place. She had assumed that everyone felt that way.

"Supporting your family should not be your burden." Lexi said, frustrated. "You were a kid."

"Why isn't it my burden, Lexi? Why shouldn't I take care of my family? You can just walk away from your life. I can't leave thousands of years of history. Of family. Of kin."

"Ross left to go to college."

"And he came back." The water was boiling. Dot stood, put tea bags in cups and poured water over the top. Handing Lexi a mug, she sat down. "Lex, you're here for, what? Seven days? Ten days?"

"I thought the oil money was helping?"

"Everyone thinks that. With oil money you can do what you want. But I have a big family, Lex. There are decades of poverty here. You know that."

Ashamed, Lexi said, "I do know that." She put her arm around Dot. "I'm sorry."

Dot seemed to accept Lexi's apology, more quickly than she thought she would. But, then again, they had been close. When they were little, Lexi, Dot, and Collette would play in the chapel and vestry in the basement, left as if there were a rapture, the people taken up to heaven leaving everything behind. It had been a Catholic hospital though no one their age could remember its past life and they never bothered to ask. Things just were the way they were.

Old crimson robes and sashes hung behind doors, dusty tables with ornate candle holders on top, even a bottle of wine was left down there. There were rooms with stainless steel gurneys that they would take turns lying on while the others wheeled them on the cold steel down the empty halls. They laughed thinking it must have been the morgue. Now, Lexi wondered how it was that anyone could live in a broken down hospital.

She was shaken out of her memories when Dot spoke again. "This is my family. This is my home." Dot stood up. "Where is your family? Where is your home, Alexandra?"

And there it was: not forgiven yet.

33

Ross provides an excellent distraction impossible to ignore.

That night, Lexi was relieved that Ross invited her out on his boat. She wanted nothing to do with grief over Brody, her disappointing Dot, Detective Reiger's pain, and was almost regretting wanting to know more about her parents.

It was warm and Lexi agreed to the boat ride only after Ross reassured her that he sprinkled catnip and basil at the bottom of the small boat to keep mosquitoes away.

She stared at the water chasing the moon's light as the boat rocked gently with the waves.

Ross steered the boat into a small alcove. They waded to the shore pulling the boat onto the rocky beach. Ross spread a blanket under a tree away from the shoreline, a sliver of moon brightened the night sky.

To keep bugs away, they gathered driftwood and "old-man's beard," a light-green lichen they used to start a fire.

Ross packed a dinner for them and spread a feast before her. Lexi was happy to see dried seaweed—it made up for the gumboot, a tough and rubbery giant mollusk that she choked down to be a good sport.

Ross gave her a wide smile. "You must like me."

"Why do you say it like that?"

"I wanted to see if you'd eat gumboot. Colette dared me to bring it. She said if you liked me, you'd eat it."

She gave him a mock look of disgust, happy that she had proven her intentions. She watched as Ross pulled a package out of the backpack and unwrapped a piece of smoked salmon. The sugary, smokey fish, a perfect union of sweet and savory.

A piece of fish, she thought.

When they were full, Lexi pulled Ross to the blanket as they gave the sky their full attention. As they lay next to each other holding hands, Ross said, "The stars–"

Lexi finished the sentence "–are looking into the past." They laughed.

When there were no clouds, the stars made Lexi feel as if the heavens were falling from the sky. It was a feeling she remembered from her childhood. A thrill and a terror running through her body as the illusion of the stars crashing into the earth scared her. She closed her eyes to stop the fear.

Ross looked at Lexi with her eyes shut tight, leaned closer to her and whispered, "What about the past are you afraid of?"

She kept her eyes closed and said, "I suppose the truth about my parents."

"Has it been painful?"

"It has. And there are questions about the crash. I suppose there was always speculation, but now I know and I can't unknow it."

He whispered, "Keep your eyes open. The stars will stop falling. They will not destroy you."

She opened her eyes and squeezed his hand.

"These are the same stars that you see in San Francisco," Ross mused.

"The stars in the city are the city." Lexi felt as if she had stopped the sky from falling. "Coit Tower, a big fire hose, the Transamerica Building, a pyramid. There's Golden Gate Bridge. The gates to Chinatown! They are the stars. Besides, there's too much light and the stars can't compete."

"I've seen pictures of San Francisco, Lex. It is beautiful and the buildings are their totem poles. It's their symbolism, I suppose. I get why you love it."

As soon as they had packed away the remains of their dinner, they shook out the blanket and sat down, each reaching for the other. Lexi caressed his warm skin, kissed his shoulders, his neck and mouth as his mouth mirrored her movements on her skin. Their clothes peeled away, their limbs entwined.

They made love under the stars, accepting the others' bodies offered up as if to the gods. Obliterating the past and the future. Only the present was known to them.

Every lover Lexi had up until Ross had taught her what she liked and what she didn't. But with Ross, there was no thinking, no mind at all. It was like music was washing over her. Sometimes it was slow and sweet like a soul song and sometimes it was staccato and steady like a drum beat accelerating into a kind of frenzy. Every time it was different and each time led to a deeper connection. They spoke less yet knew more. At last, they collapsed into each other's arms.

Ross puts his head under Lexi's shoulder. The weight of it felt good against her breast, even with the tenderness, a signal of her coming period. A fierce longing came over her. She turned her head toward his and they kissed. Not the gentle kisses of childhood friends falling in love, but the carnal lock of lust.

Ross's body had rivers of muscles. Sweat poured from him like raindrops. She explored every inch of his body as he did hers. An ocean of wetness released as they rocked and swayed like the ocean to the shore. Just as quickly as their passion had rekindled, they fell into a soft sleep.

Lexi woke, wrapped in several warm blankets. Of course, he had packed everything they needed, she thought. But where was Ross? The smell of the wood fire and coffee brought her to her elbows.

She heard rustling in the bush before she could see him. "Hello sleepyhead. I had the call of the wild." He walked to the campfire and, using a towel, picked up the coffee pot and poured the dark liquid into mugs.

Ross handed her a steaming cup.

"I don't remember you being this, I don't know, outdoorsy," Lexi said, impressed. "You preferred books."

Ross nodded. "You didn't stick around long enough for me to show you." He took a sip of coffee before leaning into her, hugging her close. She could smell pine and sweat. She kissed him, long and deep. It felt like a goodbye.

"We grew up."

Lexi smiled. "We did."

34

Lexi, knowing she has to head home to San Francisco soon, decides she either needs answers or has to let go of what happened to her parents. She brings things to a boil to force the issue.

The first order of business for Lexi was to stop thinking of Alaska as her home. She said out loud, "This is Gram's house. I am visiting."

The second thought she had looking around the room she grew up in was that Doris needed to come clean. Why had she kept everything from her? Terry's controllingness, her mother's infidelity, she knew Doris didn't know about Kak and her father so that was a non-starter. But her parents' troubled marriage was on the table.

Why was Doris so reluctant to talk about her own daughter?

Determined, Lexi went downstairs and joined Doris at the kitchen table. She asked the question. Doris took a deep breath. "I never wanted you to see how upset I was after June–" Her hands fell into her lap and she started to cry. Lexi had never seen her grandmother cry. She didn't know what to do. She looked outside at the rain. Sheets of water ran down the window as the storm battered the coast. The sound seemed to amplify her grandmother's grief. Torrents came down obscuring the trees and the docks below.

When the crying didn't stop, Lexi stood, walked behind her grandmother and placed a hand on her shoulder. Doris surprised her by grabbing her hand and squeezing. She patted her eyes dry with her apron.

"Make me a cup of coffee, Alexandra. None of that San Francisco dreck. Give me a cup that doesn't taste like motor oil."

Once the coffee was made and poured, Doris started to talk. "I always thought Terry killed them both. He was so jealous. I wouldn't put it past him to crash that plane."

Lexi stared at her grandmother.

"I can see why you never wanted to tell me that." Their eyes met and something broke. They started to laugh. A deep belly laugh that surprised them both.

35

*Lexi's new motto is "fix it or break it."
She had booked the ferry to return
home the following Monday so she
needed answers and she needed them
now.*

After a fitful night's sleep, Lexi woke, dressed and headed to the newspaper office. Doris suggested that Bob knew more about June and Terry than anyone and, like Doris, he might be leaving something out to protect her. She also remembered the check from the oil company and stuffed it into her pocket before leaving Doris' house, as she thought of it now.

Bob was on the phone when she walked in. He motioned for her to sit. He was mid-sentence:

"I don't care what they told you. I'm doing the story." He held the phone away from his ear. Lexi could hear someone screaming on the other end.

Bob winked at her as she sat down.

He kept the phone at a distance and yelled into the receiver, "I'm sorry you feel that way," and hung up, giving Lexi a mischievous grin. "Sometimes I love my job."

She returned his smile. It was hard not to appreciate Bob's enthusiasm and passion. She said, "I have to ask you something."

"Shoot." He sat up and leaned slightly forward, focused.

She pulled the check out of her pocket. "What is this?" She handed him the check before taking a seat. To her surprise, Bob laughed. "Oh this. Honestly, you have an investigative reporter in you. Your mother would have loved this."

"Bob," Lexi said, aware of his charming her. "Is this hush money? The date is right around the time professor Parker was working for that oil company."

"Technically, it was an oil company association. Sort of a front for big oil to do its research indirectly."

"So it is hush money?"

He set the paper on the desk. "I suppose it is. I should have asked for more." Bob laughed again. Lexi frowned.

"Did you notice it's not a canceled check. I never cashed it, but you're right about one thing. It was a shitty thing to do to entrap them, but that was years ago. The statute of limitations on stupid has expired. Those were wild times. Oil money made everyone crazy when it started flying around."

"Don't give me that 'last frontier' "gold rush' bull." Lexi was embarrassed. How could she not have noticed? She remembered Detective Reiger had warned her that when you're a hammer, everything looks like a nail."

Bob turned serious for a moment. "I am sorry to have disappointed you Lexi. But I didn't break the law." Bob took the check and tore it up before tossing it into the trash.

"Jeese." Lexi shook her head. She got up and walked to the door. "Why did you keep it?"

"I didn't even remember I had it." He was pleased with himself. "Plus, I didn't expect one of my best friend's daughters to be such a great investigator. Bravo to you." He smiled, put his feet on the desk, and picked up the newspaper copy.

"I have some corruption to uncover." He looked at her with a good natured expression. "Off with you."

Lexi found Ross's motorcycle with the key in the ignition where he told her he would leave it outside his parents' house. She had borrowed it to ride to the end of Brusich Road near Refuge Cove to the hangar where her parents ran their business. A bit unsteady after only one lesson, she started the engine and drove around the old school parking lot for a bit.

She wanted to see the remains of the plane and look in the office. She had hit one dead end after another. Maybe there was something there that would shed light on what happened.

The ride out of town reminded her why tourists came to this part of the world, especially on a day like today. The sky was a rare blue and cloudless, the water sparkled in the sun. Everything was green and lush.

Lexi pulled up to the old hangar. She was surprised to see that it was wide open; she walked inside feeling as ready as she would ever be to face the remains of their plane.

There it was, a long table with pieces of metal strewn on top, organized into sections. Electronic instruments in one corner. A rusty ashtray attached to an arm piece in another. Small pieces from the fuselage. To her right there were larger pieces. Engine parts were scattered on the floor. Lexi gasped when she saw a large piece of the cockpit and two crumpled seats.

Doris sat looking over the narrows, drinking her cold coffee before returning to her puzzle. The phone rang but she didn't hear it. She was thinking about the picture she was piecing together. The San Francisco skyline was a gift from Kak. She liked imagining Lexi in one of the offices, riding the cable car, living in one of the apartment buildings in the picture.

The answering machine picked up. Detective Reiger's voice fell on deaf ears. "Lexi, it's me. Pick up. Call me as soon as you get this message. I did some digging and found a restraining order your mom filed. Lexi, please if you're there, pick up."

Lexi heard someone in the back of the hangar. She darted to her left and flattened herself against the wall. She could see someone in an open door to what looked like an office. They were back lit so she could not make them out. Looking around, she found a wrench hanging on a peg board with other tools. She carefully lifted it off and moved slowly toward the office.

There was a window but the glass was too dirty to see anything except a shape inside. Lexi raised the wrench as she approached the door.

She shouted, "Who's there!" A body came hurtling toward her. It was a woman. Lexi screamed.

Emerging into the light of the hangar was Margaret.

Lexi stared at her. "You scared the living daylights out of me."

"Ditto kid!"

Lexi was still holding the wrench. "God, what are you doing with that box-end?" Margaret asked, collapsing with relief against the door frame.

"What's a box-end?" Lexi asked.

"That wrench you're wielding."

Lexi lowered the wrench.

"Don't drop it. Those are worth a fortune." Margaret reached for the tool, took it from Lexi and set it on the desk inside the office.

Once they caught their breath and were a little more calm, Margaret disappeared into the office and emerged moments later with two bottles of Coke. She set them down and cracked open the tops with an opener on her key ring. Handing her a bottle, she motioned for Lexi to follow her to the mouth of the hangar and sat down cross-legged on the dirt. Lexi did the same. They drank their sodas in silence. The air smelled of motor oil and seawater. Lexi looked across the narrows lost in thought before turning to look at Margaret who closed her eyes, soaking up the sunlight.

"What happened to my parents, Margaret?"

"I don't know, honey." Margaret's eyes were still closed. "People often come up here who are running from something. They don't call it the last frontier for nothing." She took a long drink from the bottle and looked at Lexi, her face serious but soft. "But, this is our home. It's not an escape hatch. I'm not sure there is an answer."

Lexi sat in stunned silence. This was the second time she felt the weight of it. This place that had shaped her. Margaret's resignation was a shock to her. She looked at the debris from the plane scattered deep in the hangar. All those years of piecing it together. There had to be an explanation.

Before she could respond, Margaret jumped up, extending her free hand to Lexi, helping her off the ground. She threw her empty bottle in the trash and gave Lexi a long, hard hug.

"I have the lunch shift so gotta go. Feel free to look around but don't touch my tools." Margaret was still holding onto her.

Lexi smiled and nodded.

"You are June's daughter." She said, letting go just as abruptly as she'd grabbed her. "Don't forget that."

With that, she turned and left the hangar. Lexi sat back down and finished her Coke. What was it about this tiny town that made every decision feel monumental?

Lexi heard Margaret's truck pull away.

36

Margaret and Bob discuss their growing acknowledgement that their work to find a reason for the Fagan's plane crash is futile. Maybe it was an accident.

Before heading to the bar, Margaret stopped by the Daily News to talk to Bob. She found him sitting behind his desk.

"I gotta go." He said, hanging up before standing to give Margaret a hug.

"It's good to see you," Bob said, motioning for her to sit down.

She shook her head "no" and said, "I can't stay. I just came to tell you that I saw Lexi at the hangar."

Bob almost gasped. "Did she see the wreckage?"

Margaret nodded.

"That must have been painful for her."

"It was but I think it fueled her obsession with what happened." Margaret smoothed her hair. "I don't know. Maybe I just saw, through her, how obsessed I've been for all these years."

"What do you mean?"

Margaret put her hands on the back of the chair, almost as if she needed stability. "I'm done, Bob. I can't do this anymore."

"I understand." Bob said. "I'm coming around, too. What have we accomplished? Lexi's been looking into it and coming up empty."

"It's empty, Bob." Margaret turned around, resigned, and waved as she left for work.

Lexi wanted to stay and look through the wreckage, maybe find flight records in the office. A short time after Margaret left, Lexi was throwing her Coke bottle away when she saw two of the three fuel tanks sitting on the ground under the table littered with wreckage.

Her inspection was disturbed by the sound of tires on gravel. She thought maybe Margaret forgot to tell her something. She was glad that she could ask Margaret about the tanks, the tiny pieces of one of them had been welded back together.

When Margaret didn't appear, Lexi walked outside to see who it was when she felt a sudden jerk to her hair from behind her. Off balance, she stumbled, as gloved hands curled around her neck and squeezed.

She twisted her body as hard as she could to loosen the grip. It worked. The hands let go, she heard a grunt as they separated, sending them both to the ground.

Lexi scrambled to her feet and ran as hard as she could inside the hangar, gasping for breath.

If she could make it to the office, she could lock herself inside. Whoever was behind her was gaining on her. The office door was still open, Lexi lunged as she felt a hand grab her jacket. She wriggled out, slamming the door behind her. She heard a yelp.

She frantically turned the lock on the doorknob. That's when the banging started. Lexi retreated into the small space. It was dark and she tripped over boxes, nearly falling over.

As suddenly as it started, the banging stopped. Not wanting to be seen, she left the lights off. Finding the desk, she groped around. She felt a thick layer of dust covering a stapler, a wire inbox full of papers, but no phone.

Panicked, Lexi's eyes adjusted to the dark when the sound of splintered wood made her turn away from the desk and toward the door as it split into pieces from an ax ripping it apart.

Looking for a place to hide, Lexi decided she would go down fighting. A big piece of the door broke open and a gloved hand reached in and unlocked the door. Lexi saw the wrench Margaret left on the desk. She grabbed it and brought it down hard on the arm still in the door as it opened.

A scream of pain. A direct hit as the arm recoiled. Now that the door was open, Lexi could see a figure in black with a ski-mask over the head. The body was blocking the door from fully opening. She squeezed her way past but the other arm grabbed at her leg, holding her in place.

The ax was laying on the floor, close enough for the assailant to grab if they let go of her leg. She wriggled and brought the wrench down on the arm holding her, lost her balance, and missed, landing hard on the cement floor.

The hand let go of her leg and, lifting her head, she saw her attacker grab the ax. The figure now stood directly over her.

Despite the pain in her head and body from hitting the floor, Lexi knew she had to move. She gathered her strength and kicked with all her might. Another scream, high and piercing as the figure recoiled, collapsing as the ax hit the floor with a loud clang.

Lexi struggled to pull herself up, unable to move as fast as she wanted. She stood over the figure moaning on the ground and pulled off the ski-mask.

It was Bob Kincaid.

Stunned, Lexi stared at the man crumpled on the hangar floor holding his leg. She understood in that instant what everyone had been telling her: the pull of her mother.

"You loved June." She said, sinking slowly next to Bob who was groaning and rocking back and forth.

"You broke my leg!"

"I hope I broke your arm too," She said, bitter. "You killed my parents."

"All I did was love June. Terry didn't deserve her."

They were both crumpled on the ground. Lexi wanted to get far away from him but could hardly move.

"I'm so sorry," He whispered. "I can't do this."

She said with fury, "You will do this." She managed to stand and kicked his leg before grabbing a nearby chair, setting it far enough away from Bob that he could not reach her if he got a second wind.

Bob whimpered for what seemed like a long time. Finally, he sighed and said, "I was trying to kill your father." His face fell. "God that sounds awful." He let go of his leg and put his head in his hands.

Lexi was speechless. She waited for Bob to continue. "Terry had flown that morning so he'd already done a full pre-flight check for his next flight. I think Margaret had done one, too. He needed to go into town to pick up a package. I was at the hangar. I hid my car in the woods until your dad drove off and, when he left, I sabotaged the plane."

Lexi tried to remain calm but her face flushed with anger.

As if unburdening himself, Bob kept talking. "I checked the manifest and the schedule the last time I was at the hangar earlier that week. I made up a story that took me right up the road to Totem Bight." He choked up.

"It was only supposed to be your dad flying that day. I made sure June was working for the paper. But your dad stopped by the office and picked her up to go with him. I had no idea. I never would have let her leave if I was at the office."

"I don't understand." Lexi implored. "How did you know the plane would crash? What did you do?"

"Your dad had two flights that day. One run in the morning and an afternoon flight to a remote area where the gas company was setting up the pipeline. I researched how the gas tanks worked on the Beaver. There are three fuel tanks under the plane–they're a pain to check. I knew Terry wouldn't bother checking before taking off for his second flight. He would re-fuel the first tank and never check the others. I put water in the second tank when he was gone."

"You only checked out the plane's manual after the crash." Lexi was incredulous.

"Not true." He sighed. "I checked it out earlier but made sure it was the bottom of an old card and that Johnny would be the last one to check it out after the accident on a new card."

Lexi was skeptical. "I don't buy it."

"Your dad never stopped talking about himself. I knew his entire schedule even without looking at the manifest. He told me there was a package he was picking up, where he was picking it up. Everything. I knew where he would be every minute of that day."

"The second flight was a long flight there and back, and when the first tank ran low on gas, he would have to switch tanks right where it was the most impossible to land. It's just mountains and there's no water large enough to put even a small plane down."

Bob stopped talking to catch his breath. "Why did she go with him?" he sobbed.

Lexi had heard enough. "Why did you want to kill my father? Why didn't you just tell my mother how you felt?"

"She knew." Bob became even smaller as he sat on the ground cradling his knees. "I know she loved me too before Terry swooped in."

"You're the other 'R' in her diary." Lexi felt sick.

"I can see the headline now," Bob said, his voice dripping with irony. "Obsession Takes Local Reporter to Extremes."

Lexi was not going to give him the last word. She said bitterly, "You loved my mother to death."

Later, at the police station, Lexi noticed the beaded bracelet she found when she arrived in town at the dock was missing. She must have lost it in the struggle with Bob.

With Collette's encouragement, the lead detective allowed Lexi to listen in when they questioned Bob. He told them that he knew that Lexi was at the hangar because Margaret told him.

Lexi heard how, at first, Bob was amused by Lexi's interest in her parents' plane accident. He did not take it seriously. But as time went on, he recognized how dogged she was and that she was good at figuring things out. So later, fearing she would uncover his affair with June, he told Lexi the story about the former mayor and how he had it out for her mother. When that did not stop Lexi, he had to come up with more ways to divert her attention so he fed her the information about professor Parker.

When Lexi spoke with detective Reiger, he told her he discovered that June had filed for a restraining order against Robert Kincaid just before the plane went down. It was filed in Juneau because Bob was so well connected that June needed to keep it quiet until it was ruled on. The court never had a chance to make a determination because June died. No one in town knew that June was seeking a restraining order. She had not even told Margaret.

37

Lexi says goodbye.

efore leaving for San Francisco, Lexi took one more trip to soak up her past. Recovered from her injuries, she felt the full weight of the life she had put on hold. She missed her old-lady cat and her bakery friends.

She remembered Reiger telling her that life didn't have a solution. Everything that happened to you was your life. That was evident from how detective Reiger, and later Jackie, had forgiven the man who cut Jada's life short. They accepted his acknowledgement for what he had done as what it was, a genuine request for amends.

Lexi stood in Kak's living room. There was a strong scent of Pine Sol, coffee, and Brandy? Lexi took a deep breath. Brandy.

Kak motioned for her to sit.

"What's on your mind? You don't visit unless there's something going on in there." She pointed to Lexi's head.

Lexi took a breath before beginning. "When I worked at the old folks' home, I could see that the residents' lives were like a jigsaw puzzle. It was mostly complete, maybe a few pieces missing, but as time went on, they lost more of the pieces." Lexi looked down. "I know my grandparents were old but I never put them in that box with the other old people at the home. How is Doris, really?"

"Honey," Kak said. "She doesn't know if she's on foot or on horseback."

Lexi was not sure she wanted to put the next thought into words, but Kak's response sealed the deal. "Maybe I should stay and take care of Doris?" She lowered her eyes.

Kak raised Lexi's head with her hand. "Absolutely not. You have your life to live. I'm here to take care of her. They were happy to raise you but, let's be frank, they didn't do a bang-up job did they?"

Lexi managed a smile.

"You have a lot of catching up to do."

"Go," Kak rose, abruptly. "Have a life. Have a lot of sex."

Lexi gave a weak smile.

Kak understood. "Ha! Have more sex!"

Lexi couldn't help but laugh.

"And break some hearts."

Lexi grimaced.

"That's my girl. Break some more hearts!"

Relieved, Lexi stood and hugged Kak for a long time.

At the Ferry terminal, Lexi looked into Ross's dark eyes. "You know I love you," she said.

He touched her cheek and said, "You know I love you." They kissed tenderly.

"One thing," Lexi said almost as an afterthought. "What happened to the Indian headdress?"

"I don't know." Ross smiled, mischievous, "I imagine it's with its people."

They hugged one last time before Lexi turned to walk the plank onto the ferry. Just as she reached the top and turned to wave, she saw Ross rushing past the last of the passengers until he reached her.

"I have something for you." He took a silver cuff bracelet from his pocket carved with Raven. Stunned at its beauty, she put it on. It gleamed even in the low gray light. He touched her heart with his palm. She could feel the warmth against her chest.

He said, "You're always home, Alexandra."

They kissed a long, passionate kiss before he gave her a reassuring smile, turned, and walked to the dock.

The horn blew. Lexi waved from the deck as the Ferry pulled away, Ross's last words echoing in her ears.

She smiled, closed her eyes and turned her face to the sky as fat raindrops came down, washing her clean, cleansing her of sadness. She was a woman. A woman with a before and an after.

THE END

ACKNOWLEDGEMENTS

L et me first thank Ketchikan, Alaska, my hometown and a place where the Native population has enriched the culture and given their stewardship for centuries. When I grew up there in the 60s and 70s, Native culture was not appreciated or celebrated as it is today. While I refer to the indigenous Haida and Tlingit people occasionally as "Indians," it is a reflection of the times the book takes place, the mid-1980s. References to "Native" and "Indigenous" people were not the norm at the time, but Alaskans have come to appreciate and recognize that Alaska is Indian Country and how they would like to be referred to is the norm.

My heartfelt thank you to Robert Kinerk. (I hope you enjoyed the depiction of a reporter's delightful personality and that you revel in the journey the character takes.) Robert has the enthusiasm and spark of the character in the book so it was fun to write. The real Robert is an excellent writer. If you want to know more about Alaska and read a great story, pick up Robert's latest book, "Mr. Sweetcheeks in Alaska," on Amazon. Robert also wrote the play that I talk about in the book, "The Fish Pirate's Daughter." It was a large part of my childhood as my parents and their friends put on the melodrama for tourists every summer.

Thank you to my sister, Heather, and my mother, Suzanne. They are my first readers and deserve awards for wading through the first, messy drafts of my books. I couldn't do it without their support and eagle eyes.

My childhood friend, Kara Altman, and I grew up in Ketchikan. While I moved from Alaska to the Bay Area when I was 12, Kara attended middle and high school in our hometown. She was instrumental in giving me the vibe of what it was like to go from grade school through high school in Ketchikan. I'm grateful for her wonderful descriptions that helped me flesh out Lexi's school years.

I'm also grateful to my friend, Elizabeth Meeker. She embodies the adage, "ask a producer" to do anything that needs doing. Elizabeth found the right people to explain the mechanics of how seaplanes work. A special thank you to Shane Carlson, Seattle-based pilot and owner of Northwest Seaplanes and Alaska-based pilot and instructor Burke Mees—two of the best in the biz. Without their knowledge, there would be no book.

Thank you Dave Kiffer for the information on Ketchikan bars from the 1960s through the 1980s. I picked his brain and was rewarded with great details of the bar scene that a writer can only dream of hearing – until you meet a Dave.

With deep gratitude, I thank the person that turned my writing into a book and someone I am overjoyed to call a friend, my editor Stephanie Bowen. Luckily, my friend and fan of my books, Malie Tsurunaga, agreed to be my last reader. Her enthusiasm and encouragement with a friendly, "How's the book coming?" has kept me going on more than one occasion.

And a shout out to my favorite people, artist Joseph Stoddard, writer James Grant Goldin, photographer Gina Cholick, executive stylist Kim

Apodaca, and Annie Choi, owner of Found Coffee in Eagle Rock, California. There never were better than you lot.

There is one last thank you to make in memory of my Uncle Bill Doerr—who my sister and I called Nucca Bill when we were kids—I would like to thank him in writing. After my first book, he wrote me a kind and supportive letter. In it, he told me that my grandfather had always wanted to write a mystery book which I was not aware of. And this is the get out the hanky part—Bill wrote that my grandfather, Maurie Doerr, would have been so proud of me.

If you want to know how Lexi Fagan turned into Lexi the sleuth, read book one in the series that answers the question: Where's Jerry?

BAKER'S DOZEN

Lexi is newly arrived in San Francisco

and lands a job working at McCracken's Bakery. When her lover, firefighter Jerry Stevens, turns up dead in a devastating hotel fire, Lexi has no time to mourn.

Homicide detective Robert Reiger discovers Jerry's death was no accident.

Caught up in the investigation, Lexi uncovers a shocking secret that just might get her killed.

In book two, Lexi discovers what she's made of when she gets sucked into another murder investigation.

FREE FOR ALL

Lexi finds a new job in the City by the Bay as a receptionist at a political think tank. Her life seemed to be getting back on track when her boss is found murdered in his office. Lexi's old friend, Detective Robert Reiger, pulls the young redhead into the investigation.

Lexi becomes Reiger's "eyes and ears" inside The Freedom Institute—where suspects seem to multiply by the day.

ABOUT THE AUTHOR

Autumn Doerr is a writer, podcaster, and television producer based in Los Angeles, but the Bay Area still holds her heart.

"San Francisco is where I grew up," says Autumn. "It's where I became an adult, made life-long friends and where my family still lives."